The Double Conspiracy

Richard J Sloane

The Double Conspiracy by Richard J Sloane

ISBN 978-1-970072-77-8 (Paperback)
ISBN 978-1-970072-78-5 (Hardback)

This book is written to provide information and motivation to readers. Its purpose is not to render any type of psychological, legal, or professional advice of any kind. The content is the sole opinion and expression of the author, and not necessarily that of the publisher.

Printed in the United States of America.

New Leaf Media, LLC
175 S. 3rd Street, Suite 200
Columbus, OH 43215
www.thenewleafmedia.com

<u>Warning!</u>

This file is not to be opened or read by anyone under an A+ Security Clearance, on pain of the direst penalties up to and including treason, until its contents have been declassified.

Chapter 1 –
Sunday evening

It was Sunday evening, the fag end of the week, and I was at home alone as usual, sitting on the sofa, sipping whisky and watching the late news. Since I'd lost my job, I had been alone a lot. I hated Sundays, with time seeming to drag so slowly I felt like a fly trapped in amber. They reminded me of death or, more specifically the death of my wife, Jenny, and I thought that the grieving days should really be over. So when the phone rang, I pounced on it, ready for contact with anyone, even a double-glazing salesman. But it wasn't a double-glazing salesman.

'Is that you, Jack?' I heard Peter Holloway, the secretary of the COBRA committee, say.

'Yes, what's the problem, Peter?'

'The PM wants an emergency meeting of the Committee in one hour.'

The adrenalin started flowing then, as it always does in moments of crisis, and I replied, 'Fine, Peter, I'll be there as soon as I can.'

It took me a few minutes to change out of my jeans and T-shirt into something more formal, find the car keys and my I.D. and escape from the flat. Then I was racing through the wet streets of London towards Whitehall, wondering what the flap was about. I had seen no reference to a terrorist incident on the news, the usual reason for emergency meetings of the Committee.

Luckily, I lived not far away in Westminster and arrived at about 10.30. Having parked the car in its usual reserved space, my pass was checked by the soldier on duty at the entrance of the tunnel in the Treasury and I was soon hurrying along it towards the COBRA meeting room deep in the bowels of Whitehall. If I'd turned right at the T-junction, it would have taken me right under Downing Street and up into No.10 but I wasn't doing that today and I turned left.

I was met outside the room by an aide to the PM and, having shown my pass again, was shown inside immediately. Some of my colleagues on the Committee were already there, talking rather nervously and waiting for others to arrive. Nobody seemed to have a clue what was going on. By 10.55 most of us who could make it at such short notice were assembled and the PM came striding into the room, looking like an ungainly crane with his tie flapping and his jacket unbuttoned.

He invited us to sit and then said, 'Sorry to drag you in at such short notice, gentlemen and lady,' nodding to Patricia Porchmouth, the liaison woman with the MOD, 'but it looks like we have a security problem. I received this some time today. It was in my personal mail which I have only just got round to looking at.' And he passed around a photocopy of a letter. It stated simply, 'Dear PM, we would be grateful if you could be by your phone in the COBRA meeting room at 11.00 pm this evening, Sunday, as we have some bad news for you. Please take this seriously.' It was neatly typed and unsigned.

'I need to know how it got there,' he said grimly. Then he broke off as the tele-phone warbled softly.

'Put it on the speakers, PM,' Peter said. The PM flicked a switch, picked up the receiver and said sternly, 'I don't know how you got this number but if this is a prank, I'll have your guts for garters.'

Then we heard a muffled, disguised voice, which was probably, but not certainly, a man's, say, 'Shut up and listen. We know all about your cover-up concerning the monarchy. If you don't do exactly as we say, your government will be out by this time next week. We will communicate again with our terms by letter tomorrow.' Then there was a click, the unmistakeable sound of a broken connection. I knew the conversation had been too short for it to have been traced.

The PM had gone white and seemed to age in front of our eyes. None of us knew what the hell was going on.

Then he appeared to make a decision and said, 'Thank you, everybody. You can all leave now except for Jack. Don't worry. I can handle it.'

As they all, bemusedly and rather unwillingly, filed out, looking at me askance and leaving me alone with the PM, I wondered why he had chosen me to confide in. After all, I was probably the least important member of the COBRA committee, only there because the PM had specifically asked for me when he first came to power. Sure, I knew my way around after all those years in MI5 but so did plenty of others. I guessed it must have something to do with the personal bond we had, having been friends since we were at the same Midlands grammar school. We had gone on double dates when we were courting our wives and had corresponded regularly ever since although I hadn't seen that much of him since he came to power. But there seemed to be a stronger bond of trust between us than between him and most of the people who surrounded him. On the minus side, however, I was now a middle-aged, almost-alcoholic ex-spy and I wasn't at all sure if I was the right man to help him out of this current crisis. For, from his reaction, crisis I was sure it was. But one thing was certain: I would do my damnedest to help if I could.

When we were alone, he sat back in his chair and, looking at me directly, asked, 'How long have we known each other, Jack?'

I did a rapid calculation in my head and replied, 'About 35 years, Sandy.'

'Right. And in all that time have you ever known me to be indecisive?'

'No, I can't honestly say I can,' I said, reflecting that decisive was what he had always been, even way back, when he had decided he was going to marry Sarah and become PM one day.

'Well, now I don't know what to do,' he said miserably.

'Perhaps it would help if you told me the background to all this,' I suggested.

'Yes, you're right of course,' he said, deliberating for a few seconds. 'I'm going to tell you something known only to a very few.'

I waited impatiently for him to go on.

'OK,' he said hesitantly, then more strongly. 'Do you remember the time about eight years ago when I first became PM and the Queen became quite seriously ill with a virus and the State visit of the American President had to be cancelled?'

I nodded and he continued, 'Well, it was mooted then that, if the Queen had had a double, all of the problems caused by that could have been avoided. You have probably heard that both Stalin and Saddam Hussein, among others, used doubles. I pooh-poohed the idea at first but Sir Maurice kept going on about the Monarchy being a stabilising factor in the country and what if the country did become unstable. And I, mindful of the riots and recent strikes, started to take the idea more seriously.'

Sir Maurice, I thought, my old boss at MI5, who always had his aristocratic fingers in every pie.

'So, anyway, I finally consented, with a number of provisos. A double was found and trained and used for the first time about 3 years ago, successfully I might add, when the Queen again became ill.'

A look of shock must have crossed my face for he added, 'Yes, it's true, Jack. But that's not all. Now think back to the Queen's death last September. Do you remember all the problems before that about Charles acceding finally to the throne, how reluctant he was because of Camilla and how worried the country had become about their new monarch when the Queen finally died?' I nodded again and he said, 'What if I told you that she had actually died six months earlier and that the double was used in public for that time until I deemed the country stable enough to be told that she was now dead? And, incidentally, that I was sure there wouldn't be any problems about Charles taking over?'

I gasped in horror and said without thinking, 'But it wouldn't be possible to impersonate the Queen for that length of time without anybody noticing, would it?'

'I'm afraid it would, Jack,' Sandy said sombrely.

I sat back in my chair, my head spinning with too many questions. This was clearly political dynamite and the anonymous caller, if he knew everything, was right to say that, if it ever leaked out, it would certainly be the end of the government. This was Sandy's second term in office and I knew that his majority in the Commons was getting almost too slim to be sustainable. The country, let alone the Opposition, would be outraged not to have been trusted with the truth even though I could see the strength of Sandy's arguments in favour of using a double. I could even see the country being seriously destabilised by the revelation, quite the opposite of what had been intended.

'What do you want *me* to do about your mess, Sandy?' I asked finally.

'I want you to get the traitor who leaked the information first and then stop it getting out.'

'A tall order,' I said, 'seeing how obviously professional they are. And you want me to achieve this all on my own?'

'Who else can I trust absolutely, Sandy?'

'OK. But I need some hard facts. Who else apart from obviously the Queen, yourself, Sir Maurice and the double knew about this?'

'The inner Royals, Prince Philip, Prince Charles and Camilla, who were all consulted and agreed at an early stage that it was a good idea. Oh, and also the surgeon who performed the cosmetic surgery required on the double. I can't honestly see any of them being the traitor but who knows?' He shrugged helplessly. 'I don't think anybody else knew but I could be wrong.'

'Well, I suppose they will have to be eliminated first. I'll start with the surgeon. He'd seem to be the best bet. Have you got his phone number and his address?' I said, dreading the possibility of having to interview the Royals or Sir Maurice.

'Come with me.'

We left the Committee room and walked together back through the tunnel to No. 10, thankfully not talking. I had too much to think about. There he took me upstairs to his private office, went to a safe concealed behind a painting, opened it and took out a small notebook. He dictated the name, number and address to me and I copied them into my own notebook which I kept in the inside pocket of my jacket.

Then I asked, 'Can you give me a number where you can always be contacted?'

'I'll give you my personal mobile number. Only Sarah knows it and I should be permanently available on it.'

'Good, thanks,' I said, copying it down also. 'Let me know as soon as you receive the letter.'

'Will do, Jack and thanks,' he said, gripping my hand hard. 'Don't forget you are under time constraints.'

'I won't,' I promised and with that I left, making my way back through the tunnel to the car.

As I drove home, I mused on the things the powerful would do to hang on to their power and went to bed without my usual stiff whisky, knowing I would need a clear head for what tomorrow would bring.

Chapter 2 Monday am

My sleep was interrupted by a number of violent dreams but I woke to the sound of the alarm at 7.00 and made myself a decent breakfast and a large pot of strong coffee. Then at 8.00 I rang the surgeon's house and was answered by a youngish, educated female voice saying, 'Mr Phipps-Smythe's residence. Can I help you?' I gave her my name and said I had some urgent private business to discuss with Mr Phipps- Smythe. She went away to find him and I wondered what she was. Secretary? Mistress? Wife? Housekeeper? Then I heard an urbane cultured voice say, 'Mr Phipps-Smythe here.'

'I am an emissary of the PM who has asked me to call on you about one of your old cases.'

'Can you give me a number to call you back on?'

A cautious type, I thought, and I gave him my home phone number. It was only about ten minutes later when the phone rang and the same voice said, 'I hope 10 am will be convenient. I have no other slots available today.' He had obviously rung Sandy.

'That will be fine, sir,' I said and rang off. I put his address into my Satnav – interestingly, it wasn't in Harley Street - and then decided to tart myself up for the surgeon to the high and mighty, who probably wouldn't even let me through the front door if I wasn't smartly turned out. So I had a long, leisurely shower, then dug out my one respectable suit, a clean white shirt and the soberest tie I could find before finally giving myself one last admiring look in the mirror and going down to my car.

The traffic was horrendous on a Monday morning, as I should have known, and I arrived in front of the surgeon's posh Chelsea house in its tiny mews cul-de-sac at a few minutes past ten. I went up the steps and rang the doorbell. No reply. Strange. I looked up and down the mews and could see no signs of life. The hairs on the back of my neck started to prickle as they had always done in the past when confronted with imminent danger but I ignored them, thinking that this must be one of the safest places in London and rang the bell again. Still no response so I decided to go and look round the back.

As I had suspected, there was a back gate leading into a long strip of garden. The gate was swinging on its hinges and the hairs on my neck started doing their thing again. I went through the garden and came to the back door, which was also open. Going in, I almost gagged. Gas! The smell was very strong and, as I was now in the kitchen, I looked for the cooker and located it in a corner. But it was switched off. Curiouser and curiouser. I knew I had to search the house so I took the white handkerchief I had so carefully put in my breast pocket that morning, soaked it in water from the sink and holding it over my nose and mouth, went through the closed kitchen door into the main part of the house. Then I felt the heat. Flames! They were crackling nearby. I knew I had only seconds so I went quickly down the corridor stretching in front of me, opening doors to either side of me as I went. It was in the living room at the front of the house that I discovered what I had feared I might.

It had been a beautiful Edwardian room, perfectly proportioned, but now it looked ugly. There were two bodies on the floor both beaten about the head so savagely that they were almost unrecognisable. Their blood had soaked into the Aubusson carpet and stained it deep red. One was a woman and the other a man who, from the cufflinks peeking out of his shirt with H.P.S. on them, must be the distinguished surgeon, Henry Phipps-Smythe. The stench of death was palpable, overriding even the smell of the gas.

What with that appalling sight, those smells and the heat of the flames, I could stand it no longer and, managing to open the front door, I staggered out onto the steps leading down to where my car waited patiently. I was coughing and my eyes were smarting as if I had been tear-gassed and then, remembering the bloodshed inside, I bent over and threw up my breakfast. I felt weak and knew I was in no state to drive so I tottered down to the end of the mews and into a busier road. I was looking for a taxi. Life was going on as normal here and the people around all seemed to be staring at this mad-eyed apparition with his soot-stained clothes and vomit-flecked tie. They backed away from me as if I was some kind of serial killer. And I didn't blame them.

Then I saw an empty taxi and hailed it. The driver stopped and then taking one look at me, was about to take off again.

But I pulled a couple of £20 notes out of my wallet and said hoarsely, 'Take me to Downing Street.' The driver inspected the notes carefully and then, deciding sensibly to collect a quick profit, drove off in the direction of Westminster. Doubtless he thought that the policemen on duty there would have no trouble with a lone drunk. Meanwhile, after doing my civic duty and calling the Fire Brigade anonymously, I lay back on the upholstery and considered my next step. This assignment of Sandy's was clearly more dangerous than either of us had anticipated.

Chapter 3 Monday am (cont.)

I had him drop me, not at Downing Street itself, but outside the Treasury building and I scuttled down to the basement where I found the corporal on duty. I showed my ID and then asked him to ring No. 10. He looked at me dubiously but did so while I waited impatiently, got an answer obviously to his satisfaction and opened the steel door to let me into the tunnel. Like Alice, I disappeared down it and came up inside No. 10. One of the PM's acolytes was waiting there to take me to Sandy and I followed him to his private office. I barged in and found him in conference with the Chancellor.

They both looked up in surprise and then Sandy said to the other man, 'Leave us please, Tom.' The portly figure of the Chancellor squeezed by me in the doorway, eyeing my dishevelled state with distaste, and I went in, collapsing onto one of the small sofas.

'Whatever happened to you, old chap?' Sandy asked solicitously. And then, 'You look as if you could do with a drink.'

'Yes please, Sandy.' I must have fallen asleep momentarily as, when I woke up, he was standing over me holding what looked like a whisky with a concerned look in his eyes. I downed it in one, then sat up straighter. 'What have you got me into, Sandy?' I asked.

'Tell me what happened. I presume you went to see Mr Phipps-Smythe?'

'Yes, but I found him dead in his living room with a woman beside him. They had both been murdered. But I suppose, on mature reflection, that's one less suspect to worry about,' I concluded heartlessly but immediately felt sorry for my flippant words. Then I added, 'It was clearly a professional job. Whoever's running this conspiracy must have power and money to be able to get to you so easily *and* hire a killer.'

'OK, Jack. I get the message. You're angry with me for getting you involved in something dangerous. But you're a big boy. You can take care of yourself. It still leaves us with the problem of who's involved in all this.'

I accepted the ruthless rebuke and saluted him, 'Yes, boss. You're right. Now I'm worried about the double.'

'So am I, so am I,' murmured Sandy. 'You'll need her name and address.'

'Of course,' I replied. This time he didn't need to consult his little black book but told me the name and address from memory. I thought this strange as I was writing them down and asked 'What are you keeping from me, Sandy?'

'Nothing, Jack, nothing. I promise.' I could swear he blushed, something I had never seen him do before, but in the circumstances thought no more of it.

I said, 'OK. I've been thinking about the safest place to take her to and I think Chequers would be ideal. She would be well guarded and it's very different from any of the other safe houses I know as it's not controlled by MI5 but by the Army. Remember, Sir Maurice is still a suspect.'

He looked pensive for a moment and then, in his usual decisive manner, nodded and said, 'OK. I agree. I'll set it up.'

Then I looked at the name I had written down 'Miss Pamela Burrows'. It meant nothing to me. 'OK, then, I'll get going.

One final thing, my car is still outside the surgeon's house if it hasn't been towed away for forensic analysis. I'm probably a suspect in the murders, you know. If it could be brought back to my house, and the Plod reassured that I had nothing to do with the murders, I'd be grateful. Here are the keys.'

'It will be done Jack,' Sandy said, accepting them and reaching for the phone. 'I really don't think Miss Burrows had anything to do with it. Look after her, please. She's a nice lady.'

'If she's innocent and still alive,' I replied grimly and left the room, almost bumping into the Chancellor outside who had obviously been waiting for us to finish.

I was taken back the way I had come and asked the Corporal if he could get me a taxi. While he was doing that, I went into a nearby washroom and, with liberal applications of soap and water on my clothes and my face and hands, cleaned myself up as best as I could. When I came out, I dropped the handkerchief I had used before into the waste bin. A taxi took me home where I changed into more comfortable clothes, in this case a clean T-shirt, jeans, and a comfortable jacket and gobbled a quick cheese sandwich to keep my strength up. Then I phoned Miss Burrows. The phone rang and rang but nobody picked up. I feared the worst but knew I had to go to her house to see for myself. Just then, I heard a beep from the door intercom. My car had arrived and a young man, clearly M15, stepped out. 'Did you have any problems?' I asked when we met on the stairs.

'Nothing insuperable, sir. A few arms had to be twisted, that's all.'

'Thanks,' I said as he handed me the keys.

'A pleasure to serve, sir,' he replied.

Chapter 4 Monday pm

Early Monday afternoon. A reasonable time, I thought, to visit an elderly lady. I drove to the East End where her house was situated as fast as I dared. I didn't want to get stopped by the Plod now. The Satnav got me there safely and I was soon driving slowly down her street looking for her house. It was rather a dilapidated area but some of the terraced houses sported new paint on their doors and some had even been double-glazed. Up and coming, I thought to myself. Then another thought struck me: Quite a come-down from the palace to this. I reached her front gate and noticed a child's tricycle lying in the front garden. Children? Grandchildren? I marched up to the door in my best police-man's manner, pulling my trusty police warrant card out of my pocket, and banged on it with my fist as there seemed to be no doorbell. No response. Oh, no, not again, I thought.

Then, just as I was raising my fist to bang again, a lady with curlers in her hair came out of the next-door house and asked, 'Can I help you?' 'Well, maybe you can, ma'am. I'm looking for a Miss Burrows. She has made several complaints of harassment to the police and they have sent me to ask her a few questions,' showing her my warrant card.

'She's working at the moment,' she said.

'Where?' I asked, not too eagerly.

'Down at the library,' she said, pointing vaguely down the street.

'I'm sorry, ma'am. I'm new to the area. Can you tell me exactly where it is?'

'Sure. Go down to the end of the street, turn left and it's about 200 yards down on the left. Not far.'

'Thank you very much, ma'am. I'll just pop down there and see if I can find her.'

Just as I was turning away, she added, 'There was another man here asking for her only about half an hour ago.'

My instincts went into overdrive, 'What did you tell him, ma'am?'

'Nothing. Not a dickey bird. I told him I had no idea where she was.'

'Oh, and why did you do that, if I may ask?'

'He was common, not nearly as polite as you. I sent him away with a flea in his ear. Miss Burrows likes her privacy.'

'Well, thank you *very* much,' I said in an honestly heartfelt way.

'My pleasure,' she replied and I left, walking quickly back to my car. I'm getting too old for all this running around, I thought morosely. I raced to the library, finding it easily and bounded (if that's the right word for a man of my mature years) up the steps and went into the building. There was a bored-looking girl on duty behind the check-out desk and I went up to her, showing her my warrant card, and said, 'Does a Miss Burrows work here?' She pointed a grubby forefinger to an office behind her with the door closed and a sign marked 'Private' on it. 'Would you mind getting her for me?' I asked in my steeliest voice. 'I suppose not,' she replied sulkily and went off to fetch her.

Just then, another check-out girl appeared and started looking at a computer screen. Out of the corner of my eye, I saw a youngish man wearing some sort of grey hoodie come up to her and ask in a broad South London accent, 'Miss Burrow's 'ere, is she?' At exactly that moment the door of the office opened and a trim middle-aged woman came out followed by my sulky assistant. I heard a gasp from the man next to me and then he was pulling something out from an inside pocket of his jacket. It was a gun and I reacted instinctively. I chopped my hand down hard onto his wrist and he dropped the gun in agony bending over and holding his wrist, which I had probably fractured. As he bent over, I brought my knee up hard into his face and he collapsed pole-axed onto the floor with blood gushing from a broken nose. After a second or two of shocked silence, all hell broke loose and the two check-out girls went into hysterics while others started running from the library.

I slapped one of the girls hard which stopped her screaming and told her to phone the police. Then I grabbed Miss Burrows, who had just been standing by watching events unfold, and hustled her out of the main door and out to my car. 'Get in,' I said roughly.

She didn't and I looked at her more closely. I assumed she was in shock and moved to help her in. But she said in a most equable voice, 'I'm afraid I don't get into cars with strange men. Can't you introduce yourself?'

'My name's Jack and I've been sent by the PM to get you to a safe place,' I replied apologetically.

'Oh well, that's OK, then,' she said ironically, hopping nimbly into the car and showing a nicely–turned ankle in the process.

I drove off fast, my Merc responding well to my footwork, and soon we were out of the East End heading west. I had been keeping a close eye on the mirror watching out for tails and then turned to my kid-napee and handed her my mobile phone, saying 'I need you to make a phone call for me.' I gave her Sandy's number which she dialled, handing the phone back to me.

As soon as he answered, I said, 'I've got her, Sandy, and we're on our way to the place we agreed. We had a bit of trouble at her workplace. There's an injured man there. I would like him picked up by the police asap if it hasn't already been done and handed over to Sam Bullock, the DCI at Scotland Yard, who I know and trust. Tell him he had a gun so it shouldn't be difficult to charge him and to look after him carefully as I'll want to talk to him soon.' I heard the grunt of agreement and continued, 'There is one other little thing you could do for me. We seem to have acquired a tail. A black powerful-looking bike being ridden by a guy with one of those black-out visors. Could you have him picked up quietly and also handed over to Sam?' 'Will do, Jack,' came the reply, 'stay on the line. Where are you now?' 'On the Finchley Rd, heading north.' I heard the click of disconnection. Then a couple of minutes later, the phone rang again. I picked it up and Sandy said, 'Continue on the Finchley Road. Don't turn off onto Hendon Way. Your chap will be picked up shortly.' 'Thanks,' I said, keeping an eye on the black bike tucked behind a van following us.

He had picked us up before we'd even left the East End, showing that the baddies in all this were determined and resourceful. But at least he'd made no attempt to attack. When we came to the fork, I continued straight on and saw in my mirror a police car pull out from a side road and wave the bike down. Hopefully, that'll be the end of our troubles for a while, I thought, wondering briefly about the extent of the PM's powers and those of the people after us and how they compared.

I got back on to the A 406 going west and relaxed a bit, seeing nothing else to worry me. Then I remembered my passenger who had been sitting next to me having said nothing since we left the library. She must have seen me relax because she now said, 'Can I ask two questions, please?'

'Go ahead. Although I can't promise to be able to answer.'

'First, where are we going?'

'To Chequers, the PM's country residence.'

'Goody', she said girlishly. 'I've not been there.'

'And your second question?'

'Who are these bad men who clearly want to harm me?'

'I don't know yet,' I replied truthfully.

After this, she relapsed into silence again and I glanced at her, taking her in properly for the first time. She was a handsome woman, in her full prime, and looked only superficially like the elderly Queen who had so recently died. This baffled me. How could she be the double? Had I kidnapped the wrong woman?

Chapter 5 Monday evening

The rest of the drive went by uneventfully and in silence, both of us wrapped up in our own thoughts. When we got to Chequers, the corporal on duty saluted, having checked my ID, said, 'We've been expecting you, sir,'and opened the gates. I looked at my watch, only 7.45; so much had happened since I had been summoned to the Committee last night. I drove to the back entrance where I found the major-domo, a huge, apparently unflappable, ex-marine called Joe who was waiting for us. I introduced him to Miss Burrows and she graciously shook his hand. Then I asked him to take her to her room and to direct me to a secure phone. He took me to a small empty office on the ground floor and left me alone.

I phoned Sandy who answered quickly and said 'She's here, Sandy. No more problems. Thanks for sorting out the motor-bike rider. Any news on the letter?'

'Yes,' he replied. 'I got it about an hour ago. I'll read it to you: "Dear PM, Please deposit £5 million in an account of our choice. We will give you instructions on how to transfer it in the next few hours. Stay by your phone and have pencil and paper ready. If this is not done precisely as per our instructions, we will release the information we have about the double, and the cover-up by the government, to the newspapers. Yours sincerely etc." It's unsigned'.

'Interesting', I said. 'It sounds like a straightforward criminal conspiracy, however well-organised and ruthless they are. It should make it easier for us to track them down.'

'I just hope you're right, Jack,' said Sandy

'You know you're going to have to think seriously about releasing the £5 million, don't you?'

'I'm only too well aware of it.' Sandy replied. 'Meanwhile, I presume you're going to have a little chat with Miss Burrows?'

'You're damned right I am,' I said.

'Go easy on her, Jack. I can't believe she's involved.'

'After the attempt on her life, I don't believe it either but maybe she can help us. I've got to ring Sam Bullock now. Keep in touch. You know where I am.'

'Will do, Jack,' Sandy said and broke the connection. I immediately rang my old friend in the Met, Sam, who, in spite of the lateness of the hour, was still in his office.

'Have you got my two miscreants, Sam?' I asked.

'Jack, how good to hear from you. What the hell are you mixed up in?' he said in his lugubrious Yorkshire brogue.

'Just answer my question, Sam'.

'OK,' he said wearily. 'I'm afraid not is the answer but there is one thing that might help you.'

'Tell me what happened'.

'The chap we found in the library is dead, I'm afraid.'

'What?' I gasped. 'I didn't hit him that hard.'

'I know you didn't, Jack. He was relatively OK when we picked him up at the library but when the locals got him to the police station where he was to be charged, somebody walked up to him as cool as a cucumber and shot him twice in the head. He then escaped on foot. The local police were so shocked that I'm afraid a reliable description of the shooter is beyond them.'

More inexplicable mayhem, I thought. 'Do you know who the assailant in the library was?'

'Yes, but it's a dead end. He was a contract killer from South London who was actually Northern Irish. He learnt his trade in the Troubles there. Unfortunately there has never been enough evidence to put him away. He was a pro, Jack. We're better off without him on the streets.'

'Any idea of who his employer was?'

'None at all. We're working on it but I suspect he was phoned, told where to go and offered a lot of money to do the job.'

'OK. That just leaves the motorbike rider. I presume the one thing that might help me is to do with him?'

'You're right. We put a lot of pressure on him and when he broke, he told us that he had been phoned and offered five grand to follow you and report back to an anonymous phone number where you went.'

'You got the phone number, I hope?'

'Of course. It's in a disused warehouse in the East End. We went there and it was completely empty but I've left a couple of good men to watch it discreetly.'

'Good work,' I said abstractedly, thinking it was in all probability another dead end. Then I asked, 'Did he have to check in at any particular time?'

'No, only after he had found out where you were going. Unfortunately, there's an answering machine attached to the phone which can be accessed from any phone anywhere.'

'Damn', I said heatedly, 'Not much use then.'

'Probably not,' he admitted. 'And we had to let him go. Can you tell me anything, Jack?'

'Just that I'm working directly for the PM on this one, Sam.'

'I already knew that. But never mind. I like mysteries. Now there is one thing you can do for me, Jack.'

'Tell me,' I said.

'Reassure me that you really had nothing to do with the murder of an eminent surgeon and his wife this morning. I have been given assurances from on high that you had nothing to do with it but I would like to hear it from your own lips if that's OK by you. It's just that a number of people have told us that they saw a man running away from the area who bears a remarkable resemblance to your good self and your car was found outside the premises.'

'No, Sam. It wasn't me. I suspect it was the guy in the library. It's true I was in the house but they were already dead. I just wanted to ask the surgeon a few questions. By the way, that reminds me. What was the origin of the gas? The cooker in the kitchen was switched off.'

'OK, Jack. I believe you but it would probably be a good idea to lay low for a while. The murders have stirred up a hornet's nest of interest from the newspapers. To answer your question, the main pipe leading to the gas metre had been cut. It was a professional job, Jack.'

'Interesting', I said for the second time that evening. The word 'professional' kept cropping up. 'Well, thanks Sam. I'm sure I'll be in touch soon.'

'Anything I can do, Jack, I will. But you seem to be mixed up with some pretty dangerous types. Go carefully.'

'I will, don't worry,' I said and rang off. I knew it was time to speak to Miss B. but the rumble in my stomach reminded me that I hadn't had time to eat since breakfast that morning. I called Joe on the internal line and he appeared like a genie out of a bottle.

'How's Miss B.?' I asked.

'She seems OK considering,' he said. 'Any idea how long she'll be staying?'

'How long's a piece of string, Joe,' I replied enigmatically. 'Any chance of some grub?'

'Of course, sir,' he replied respectfully. 'What do you fancy?'

'How about a nice fry-up?' I said.

'Give the chef ten minutes. Where do you want to eat?'

'In here's fine, Joe.' With a wave of his hand he disappeared and I sank into thought. Exactly ten minutes later chef appeared with a delicious-looking fry-up including all the trimmings. I thanked him and ate fast and greedily. When I'd finished, I left the office, feeling much better, and went up to Miss B's room. I knocked and she bade me come in. There was a tray of tea and sandwiches, untouched, on a small table. I pointed at it and asked, 'Aren't you hungry?'

'No, thanks. I've been waiting for you to come and visit me, Jack. First, don't you think that, since I know who you are, you could perhaps find it in yourself to call me Pamela?'

'OK, Pamela,' I said uncomfortably, thinking of all the questions I wanted to put to her. I wasn't quite sure how to begin so I said, 'How do you feel after nearly being killed today?'

'OK, thanks. Although I would feel much better if I had some of my own things here. You hauled me off just with the clothes on my back and not even my handbag.'

'Sorry, very remiss of me. I'll ask Joe to rectify that the second I leave.'

'How long am I going to be here?' she asked then, echoing Joe's question earlier.

I remembered that *I* was the one who was supposed to be asking the questions but managed to answer, perhaps rather brutally, 'It's for your own safety. Remember the guy in the library. He wasn't about to kiss your hand and ask for your autograph. Then think of the guy who tried to tail us. You've got some determined people after you.'

She looked abashed for a moment, then said simply, 'Sorry Jack. I expect you want to ask me some questions.'

'Indeed, I do, Pamela.' Her name came easier this time. This was more like it. 'First, were you *really* a double for our dead Queen?' She looked shocked at the directness of the question. Then she replied,

'Since you really do seem to have the PM's confidence, I was, yes.'

'But how can that be possible? You're about 40 years younger than she was.'

She burst into peals of girlish laughter and then, through her giggles, managed to say 'A typical man's question. You should know Jack that making a woman older is easy with a little make-up. The hard part is making her look much younger convincingly.'

'But what about the voice?' I persisted.

She nearly burst out laughing again but then said in a perfect imitation of the old queen's voice, 'Young man, don't you know that us old actresses have a certain facility with accents and voices? Where on earth have you been all your life? And please address me as either Your Majesty or Ma'am depending on the formality of the situation,' wagging an apparently cross royal finger at me.

I was astounded and amused at the same time. It was positively uncanny and I only just managed to resist the temptation to get up, bow and apologise. 'So you were an actress once?' I asked.

"Ole in one, mate', she replied in pure Essex.

I realised that she had answered my most pressing question more than adequately. I hadn't kidnapped the wrong person, thank God. Then I asked my second question, 'Can you describe your recruitment for me, please? And enough of the voice, thanks.'

She smiled again and said in her normal voice, 'It was quite a long time ago, you know.'

'Just what you remember will do, thanks.'

She paused, marshalling her thoughts and then said, 'Well, I remember sitting at home alone one evening when I had a knock on my door. I had few visitors at that time (or indeed, since) and wasn't expecting anyone. So I asked who it was. 'Mr Perkins on government business, ma'am,' was the reply. I asked him to slide his ID card under the door and, damn me, if it didn't have a royal coat of arms on it with M15 written in big red letters along the top. I knew I wasn't in trouble with anybody, so, intrigued, I opened the door. Mr Perkins was quite short, had sandy hair and looked fit. He told me that Sir Maurice, the head of M15, would like to see me. I asked if I could telephone him to check that everything was kosher and he gave me a number. When he replied, Sir Maurice said that he had a mission for me of the highest importance for the country. So, being a patriotic soul at heart, I went with Perkins down to this beautiful mansion in Kent somewhere and met Sir Maurice. The first thing I had to do was to sign the Official Secrets Act which absolutely forbade me to say anything about the mission to anybody. I suppose I've broken that now, haven't I?'

She smiled at me and I smiled back saying, 'Don't worry. It's too late for all that mumbo-jumbo now,' and signalled to her to continue her story.

'Well, when I was told what I had to do, initially I was flabbergasted. I asked what on earth the point of the exercise was and he explained that the government were worried about potential instability in the country if the Queen wasn't seen out and about. That made some kind of sense. She was very elderly after all. Then I asked, 'Why me?' He told me that they had thoroughly investigated hundreds of potential ex-actresses and I fitted the bill best. I was flattered obviously. Then he told me to go home, act normally and wait for the call to begin my training. So I went home, excited at the prospect of actually using my old skills again.' She stopped and looked at me.

'Tell me about your training,' I said.

'Well, I was taken in a car with blacked-out windows somewhere deep in the country. I never found out where it was. There I was coached by a team of people in all the arts I would need: deportment, protocol, history and, especially voice. They were good to me, I must say, and I studied hard. After about 6 weeks, I was told I was ready. And I met Sir Maurice again who told me I would be re-located and found a new job. I was fed up with my old job anyway, as Sir Maurice already seemed to know – he knew an awful lot about me, by the way – and I had no ties to my old part of London. So I was posted off to my new house which I found more than adequate and told to start my new job in the library, which I duly did.

Then, about a month later, I was summoned by Sir Maurice again and told that I was going to meet the inner circle of the Royal Family who would finally vet me for the job. So I preened myself up a bit and was taken to Sandringham where I was let in by a back door. Sir Maurice was waiting for me and he took me to a smallish, comfortable living room where I met the

Queen, Prince Philip, Prince Charles and Lady Camilla. The Queen was very gracious and asked me a few questions, then said, 'You know why you're here, Pamela. Why don't you pretend to be me for the rest of the conversation?' So I put on my Royal voice and mannerisms and I think they were all quite impressed, even a bit startled. Eventually the Queen turned to Sir Maurice and said 'She's good, isn't she?' and he replied, 'She's ready, ma'am.' And the rest of the Royals agreed that I would indeed be able to do the job. So I left, went home and waited again. A few months later, the Queen got ill and I had to stand in for her. Everything went well and then, when she died, I was asked again to do the job and I presume you know the rest.'

Indeed I didn't and still had many questions for her but I restricted myself to asking how many people knew of the deception.

She replied 'The team who coached me, Sir Maurice, the PM, the Royals obviously and now you. I think that's the lot.'

No mention of the surgeon, I noticed. But I thought he could wait. 'OK, Pamela. That's all for now,' I said. 'I think you should eat now. You need to keep up your strength.'

She said, 'You know what, all that talking has made me hungry. I think you're right'. And she started devouring the plate of sandwiches which had been left for her.

She had given me much to think about and I went back downstairs pensively. I entered the office and dialled Sandy's number. As usual he was there and I told him I had an initial interview with Pamela but I wasn't satisfied. For one thing, it had all been too glib, as if it had been rehearsed for a play. But she *had* explained the central mystery of how she was able to imitate the dead Queen to a fault. I didn't think she was honestly part of a criminal conspiracy but why hadn't she mentioned the surgeon? Then I told him about her coaching team who also knew about the deception and added that it widened the net of possible traitors.

He said 'I suppose this means that your next port of call should be Sir Maurice?'.

I sighed and said very reluctantly 'Yes, I suppose so. Any news at your end?'

'I've spoken to the Governor of the Bank of England and told him about the money. I stressed that it was a matter of National Security and he agreed to lend the government the money.'

'Good,' I said. 'Can you set up the meeting with Sir Maurice for me about lunchtime tomorrow? I want to speak to Pamela again before I go.'

'Will do.' We said our goodbyes and hung up. It was late now but I wasn't tired. I went and found Joe and asked if he could provide me with half a bottle of decent whisky. I knew that more than that would impair my judgement tomorrow. He reappeared like the magician he was, holding a half bottle of single malt. I took it up to my room and sipped it slowly while organising my questions for the next day. Then I collapsed into bed and slept rather fitfully for the rest of the night, having at least one nightmare along the way. It was one I was all too familiar with. Jenny and I were punting on the Cam when suddenly the punt overturned and I could see her body being eaten by piranhas until she was only a skeleton. I woke up sweating after that and it took me ages to get back to sleep.

Chapter 6 Tuesday am

In spite of my restless night, I got up feeling refreshed and more determined than ever to get to the bottom of this ever-increasing pile of mysteries. One thing I was sure of: they were all connected somehow. I had breakfast delivered by a smiling Joe who said that Miss B. was up and eating also. As soon as I had finished getting myself ready, I went across the hall and knocked on her door.

'Hi, Jack,' she said breezily. 'More questions?'

'Just a few, Pamela. First, do you have any children or grandchildren? The reason I ask is because I saw a tricycle lying in your front garden.'

She laughed her light, silvery laugh, which I was beginning to find infectious, and said, 'No, I don't. That was put there by MI5 as a prop to make my life seem even more normal than it usually is.'

'OK. Second, what about the make-up artist who must have done the job on the two occasions you were called in to act as the Queen. What happened to her? Where did she come from?'

'Actually, she was only used at the Farm, as the MI5 agents called it. She was one of the team there. After that, I did it all by myself. Once I had been shown how, it wasn't particularly difficult.'

'Fair enough,' I said, thinking how easily she answered my questions. Was this all rehearsed? I had saved the sucker punch until last. 'And can you explain please why you didn't mention the surgeon who did the cosmetic job on you and who, I have on good authority, was also in on the plot?'

She frowned, concentrating, and then said slowly, 'I had forgotten all about him. Isn't that strange?'

'Very,' I said and left it at that. Then I got up to go and said, 'I have to leave now. I'm going to see Sir Maurice.'

'Give him my best,' she said.

'I'll be sure to do that. Please don't go wandering off. Remember your life is my and the PM's first priority.'

'I'm flattered,' she said smiling. 'Can I have a gun?'

'No way,' I said brusquely. Then, just as I reached the door, I remembered something else I wanted to ask.

'Oh, by the way, when did you first meet the PM?'

Now there was genuine hesitation which intrigued me.

'It …. It must have been shortly after I had been cleared by the Royals.'

I wasn't going to push her on it but I knew that she was hiding something, whether voluntarily or involuntarily I wasn't sure. I felt, however, that it had nothing to do with the conspiracy. 'OK. Bye then.'

'Bye', she said to the closing door.

I went down to find Joe and told him to keep a close eye on his guest and also to provide her with some clothes and personal stuff, which I had forgotten to do the night before. Then I got into the car and phoned Sandy on my mobile.

'Sleep well?' he asked.

'OK.' I replied shortly. 'Everything fixed up with Sir M.?'

'Yes, did you get anything else from Pamela?'

'She's filled in a few holes. That's all.'

'I've ordered the money to be wired to the account number I was given, which I received last night. But we need it back again, Jack.'

'Very sensible. I'm doing my best, Sandy.'

'I know you are. Good luck with Sir M. Keep in touch.'

'I will. Bye.' Short and sweet. No words wasted. That was Sandy all over and one reason why I liked him.

Chapter 7
Tuesday pm

I started the long drive down to Kent with the questions I wanted to ask Sir Maurice fixed in my mind and, after checking for tails and finding none, managed to relax and enjoy the drive. I arrived at Sir Maurice's imposing, 16th century, manor house around 12.15 and, having been checked at the gates, went up the drive and rang the doorbell. I was, I knew, bearding the lion in his den. Sir M. had been my mentor way back when I had first joined MI5 and I respected and feared him in equal measure. I knew he could be totally ruthless in his concern for his country and that he was a dangerously wily old bird but I also knew that there was a deep core of decency underneath his occasional flashes of seemingly random cruelty. He was the one who had fired me for my drinking and I knew him well. However, he knew me better and it was with some trepidation that I knew I was there to accuse him of being a traitor, even though I didn't believe it for a moment.

He opened the door himself with his usual bonhomie and invited me into his study, a large book-lined room with a big empty desk at one end with a computer on it and a grand piano at the other which he played when he was feeling out of sorts. Rather well, I remembered gloomily.

'So what can I do for you, young Jack?' he asked. No mention of the sacking. It was as if it had never happened. I knew he knew why I was there and made no reply. 'A drink, maybe?'

'Yes, please, a malt whisky will do fine.' Exactly the same ritual as we had performed many times in the past. He poured it from a crystal decanter and I knew it would be the best money could buy. And it was. I sat back contentedly in my soft leather armchair cradling the whisky and then remembered why I was there. And I remembered also his techniques for softening people up so that they would do what he wanted. I sat up straighter and asked in an equally friendly tone, 'What can you tell me about the plan to substitute the Queen with a double?'

He sighed and said, 'You must know most of it if you are asking that question.'

'Not enough. Give me your version of events.'

He seemed to open up and told me about Pamela, how he had found her and what happened subsequently. All more or less exactly as Pamela had told it to me.

'Can I see her file?' I asked.

'All the relevant documentation was destroyed,' he said.

'I know you keep your own copies of files on your computer,' I said, waving a hand at the machine standing on the empty desk.

'OK,' he sighed, walking up to the computer with me following closely. He typed a few rapid keystrokes and, lo and behold, a fairly up-to-date picture of Pamela appeared.

'Leave me please, Sir Maurice,' I said firmly.

He graciously accepted defeat and, shoulders slumped, left the room saying, 'I'll be in the living room.'

I skimmed through dozens of files detailing everything from her school reports to university, her ex-lovers, medical history and bank statements, all the way up to the present day. I felt I was prying but knew it had to be done. I was astounded by the amount of detail until I remembered the awesome power of the government to find out anything and everything about anybody they were interested in. But I noticed a discrepancy. There were six years in her CV unaccounted for. So I looked back at the names of all the files again and found one hidden amongst the plethora of others. It was simply titled PB MOD. Curious, I opened it and was astonished once again. It was marked Top Secret and detailed operations and secret missions she had been on in many of the world's hotspots. She had been in the SAS! This explained why she had been so calm when confronted by the gunman. She could probably have taken him out more efficiently that I had done. It also explained why she was chosen by Sir Maurice. She had already been vetted to the very highest level and he knew that she would obey orders without question in the interests of the country. Why hadn't she mentioned it, I wondered. Then I realised I hadn't asked her and she would have thought it irrelevant anyway.

One mystery solved and only one more to go, based only on a hunch. I called Sir Maurice back in from the living room where he was calmly reading a newspaper and asked bluntly, 'Did you hypnotise the memory of the surgeon out of her?'

He sighed again and said, 'Well guessed, young Jack. Yes, I did. For very good operational reasons. She was more scared of the surgery than anything else to do with the plan and I thought it best that she had no memories of it.'

'And did you coach her in her story?'

'Yes, again, under the influence of hypnosis. I know it was unethical but, like I said, I thought it was for the best.'

'Unethical!' I exploded. 'It was downright criminal.'

'I already told you, Jack. I thought it best for the country. Do you want an apology?'

'It's her you should be apologising to, not me,' I said angrily. Then I remembered the most important question of all. 'I understand that only yourself, Miss Burrows, the PM, the team at your place in the country and the Royals were fully apprised of the plan. Is that true?'

'Yes,' he replied simply.

'And where's the team now?'

'Perkins has been reassigned to the embassy in Afghanistan. The rest of the team are scattered all over the place. But I would stake my life on every one of them.'

And I believed him, 'So that only leaves you,' I said. 'Did you leak the information to the bad guys?'

'I assumed when I heard from the PM that that was what must have happened and I've been waiting for the question. The answer is simple. No, I didn't. I had no reason to. It was my plan after all. I wanted it kept secret more than anybody.'

I knew he could lie without batting an eyelid if he wanted to but I also believed him on this too.

'OK,' I said. 'But, given the fact that the surgeon is now dead and assuming it's not one of the Royals, how *did* it get out?'

'Yes, I read about the death of the surgeon and I've been thinking about that. I believe it could have been done at No. 10. That was where all the secret meetings took place both before and after Miss Burrows was recruited. If a high-ranking member of his own staff had wanted to bug them, for example, I don't think it would have been impossible.'

I thought about it and realised he was right. I needed to speak to Sandy right away. I asked if I could use the telephone on the desk which I knew was secure. He said yes and left me alone again to make the call.

I dialled Sandy and got straight through. 'Listen carefully, Sandy,' I said. 'I've cleared both Miss B. and Sir M. to my satisfaction but he had an idea. He suggested that the leak might have come from within No. 10.'

'Oh, no!' Sandy gasped.

'I'm afraid it's a possibility we have to consider. Where did the secret meetings about the operation take place?'

'In the most secure room in No. 10. It's in the basement and supposed to be bug-proof.'

'OK,' I said, thinking hard. 'How often is it swept?'

'Twice a day, I'm told.'

'And to whom are the sweepers responsible?'

'The Cabinet Secretary, Sir Edward.'

'Could you get a team of independent sweepers to go in and check it?'

'Yes, no problem.'

'OK. Ring me back on my mobile as soon as you have the results. I'm coming straight back to London.'

'Will do,' and we both hung up.

I went back into the library and Sir Maurice jumped up eagerly. I said, 'I have to return to London. But something else has just occurred to me. What about people at the Palace? Surely they must have known that Pamela was a double? Servants and others?'

'Yes, that's true. As well as the doctor who signed the death certificate. But they were all vetted to the very highest level and, in addition to that, I put the fear of God into them.'

I knew he could do that with no problem at all and felt sorry for the poor bastards for a moment. 'OK. Thanks.'

'Can I help with anything else?' he asked, almost plaintively.

I knew how devastated he must feel being left out of the loop on a major crisis like this, especially one of his own making, but I couldn't involve him – yet. 'No, thanks. You've already been a great help.'

'Does that mean I'm cleared?'

'In so far as I'm concerned. I can't answer for Miss B. When she finds out she was hypnotised against her will, she may decide to bring a lawsuit against you.'

I left him looking pensive and went back to my car, remembering to leave my mobile switched on.

Chapter 8 Later Tuesday

About halfway back to London my mobile trilled and I pulled over and connected. I heard Sandy's voice sounding excited. 'You were right, Jack! The sweepers found a sophisticated bug in the light switch. They said it wouldn't have been detected on a normal sweep. I have it in front of me now. Well done!'

'Good,' I said. 'We're getting closer. I'll probably be another three quarters of an hour or so. Don't do anything till I get there. And try to act normally, especially around Sir Edward. But if you could get him out of his office for half an hour or so and get a team of police searchers in to look for recording equipment, that would be useful. Don't use MI5.'

'Will do, Jack. But surely it can't be Sir Edward?'

'You never really know people, especially when they are under pressure,' I said cynically.

I drove to London as fast as I dared. It was now late afternoon, Tuesday, and the traffic was bad but this gave me the chance to think about Sir Edward. I had only met him a couple of times and considered him a typical example of the Establishment, arrogant and much too suave for my liking. But then, considering that he came from a long line of Bishops and High Court Judges, I suppose he had every right to be arrogant. I knew he had been in office for some time before Sandy became PM and I wondered what earthly reason he could have for blackmailing the PM to the tune of £5 million. He did, after all, come from Old Money. A secret vice? Quite possible, given his Public School education, thought I, the grammar school boy with a chip on his shoulder.

My speculations stopped as I arrived at my old parking spot in the Treasury. I showed my ID, hurried down the tunnel and came up inside No. 10. There I met an aide who took me to Sandy's office where he was signing official papers under the watchful eyes of another aide, surrounded by empty coffee cups. He shooed the aide out and we sat in two comfortable arm chairs. He looked at me over the top of his glasses and said, 'Well, Jack, unfortunately it looks as though you were right about Sir Edward. He *did* have some recording equipment locked away inside the bottom drawer of his filing cabinet. By the way, we were lucky with the man himself. He left work early. Some kind of family emergency, I understand.'

'Show me the bug,' I said. He brought a tiny device out of his pocket. I didn't recognise it but didn't expect to, knowing that I was a few years behind in the technology. But I knew it must be short-range. 'OK. Now the recording equipment,' I said. He went to his desk and took a small recorder out of a drawer, about the size of a mobile phone. 'Let's test it,' I said. And I switched it on, making sure that the batteries were charged. Then I went out into the corridor outside, which was empty, and whispered a few words into the bug. I went back into the office, pressed Rewind and then Play. My words came back as clear as a bell.

'Well, I guess that's pretty conclusive then,' I said.

'But why?' Sandy almost wailed.

'I suggest you get a team of accountants onto his financial affairs. Go over them with a fine toothcomb. Tell them whatever you like, maybe that he's scared his bank accounts are being accessed illegally and he's turned to you for help. They will probably need to work through the night.'

Sandy seemed relieved that something was being done about this new nightmare and said, 'OK, Jack. Anything else?'

'Yes, a couple of things. First I'd like to see this 'secure' room for myself.'

'Follow me,' Sandy said. We went down to the basement and along a corridor, then came to a heavy steel door with a complicated access code on it which opened to Sandy's instructions. We continued into a featureless room with no windows, empty except for a conference table and six chairs. 'My experts tell me that the walls have some kind of special titanium mesh in them which prevents all bugging access from outside.'

'But not from inside,' I said grimly. 'But I can see how you would feel secure in here. What time does Sir Edward get in in the mornings?'

Sandy seemed startled by the change of subject but then said, 'About 8.30, I think.'

'I want him arrested the moment he's inside his office. It'll be more discreet there.

Then I want him carefully watched until 9.30 or so. That'll give him time to stew a bit. If he could be brought down to this room around that time, we'll be waiting for him here. Oh, yes, and take his mobile off him.'

'Do you want just the two of us to interview him?' Sandy asked.

'Unless you want even more people to know about the operation, yes,' I replied.

He looked chastened. 'OK, Jack. Your orders will be carried out.'

'I don't think there's much more we can do tonight,' I said. 'Let's both try to get some rest. Can I stay here tonight?'

'Yes. Of course you can. I'm looking forward to seeing Sarah and the kids. I haven't seen enough of them the past few days.'

'I'll see you tomorrow morning, Sandy.'

'Order whatever you want,' he said as we parted upstairs.

'Thanks,' I said as I headed off to my old room whenever I had stayed at No. 10 in the past, which was, fortunately, unoccupied. It was now just before 9.00 according to my watch and I was tired. But I was also hungry. I remembered that I hadn't had lunch again and ordered a meal and a small bottle of whisky from the trusty chefs in the kitchen. I ate at a leisurely pace for a change and then watched some mindless TV while sipping the whisky. I turned in at about 10.30 and slept the sleep of the just.

Chapter 9
Wednesday am

I was woken at 8.00 as I had requested, feeling refreshed and knowing that I had needed that much sleep. I'm getting too old for this sort of thing, I thought sourly again. Then I showered, put on some clean clothes I had brought with me and had a light breakfast. I was ready to meet Sir Edward or at least as ready as I'd ever be. There was a knock at the door. It was Sandy, also looking less drawn than the night before.

'How are those financial experts getting along?' I asked, not bothering with the social niceties.

'I haven't heard anything from them yet,' he said. And he dialled a number on his mobile. He listened briefly to a report on progress, then said, 'As quick as you can, please,' and hung up. Then he turned to me saying, 'They are making slower progress than they expected. Apparently

Sir Edward's affairs are more complicated than they have any right to be.'

'We'll just have to do without them,' I said.

We went down to the basement room and I looked at my watch. 9.25.

'Wheel him in,' I said.

Sandy dialled an internal number this time and quickly gave the orders. Sir Edward duly appeared looking unusually flustered, a slim, upright figure about ten years older than Sandy or myself.

He immediately started blustering, 'What the hell's all this about, PM?' he said. Then he noticed the equipment on the table in front of us. His face went white and I thought for a moment he was going to faint.

'I think you've got some explaining to do, don't you, Sir Edward?' said Sandy.

He slumped into a chair opposite us and whispered something neither of us could hear.

'Speak up, man!' ordered Sandy in his most military voice.

We saw him pull himself physically together and a little of the old fire came back into his eyes.

'I have nothing to say,' he said.

'Oh, I think you do,' said Sandy. 'Why in God's name have you ruined everything you worked so hard for?'

Then I saw the fire go out of his eyes again and Sir Edward just crumpled in front of us, a beaten, dejected old man.

'I'm not saying anything,' he repeated in another whisper.

'Do you really want me to put the dogs on you?' I said, referring to the MI5 interrogators.

'Do what you have to do,' he replied defiantly.

'Were you doing it on behalf of anyone else?' I asked.

'I'm not saying anything,' he repeated again miserably.

'You know we'll get it all out of you in the end. Why not make a clean breast of it now and we'll take into account any extenuating circumstances?' Me as the father confessor.

No reply. He just stared dully down at the table.

'Oh, get rid of him, Sandy,' I said disgustedly.

Sandy called the two burly guards who had brought him down and they took their prisoner away with me admonishing them to keep their charge safe.

When we were alone, Sandy said, 'How far does that get us?'

'Quite a long way, actually.' I said. 'We've plugged the original leak and I'm sure that something will break soon.'

Just then, Sandy's phone rang and he answered it. He listened intently, first with incredulity and then anger. After he had hung up, he said, 'Your intuitions were right. Something *has* broken. That was the financial guys. They say that Sir Edward is basically broke and he owes £3 million to a gambling syndicate. At least he *was* broke until £5 million was paid into an off-shore account anonymously yesterday owned indirectly by him. The self-same account we paid the money into. So there's our traitor!' he finished triumphantly.

'I wondered whether he had some sort of secret vice,' I said. 'Gambling is terribly addictive.'

'Well done, Jack. You did it!' Sandy exclaimed, clapping me on the shoulder.

'Yes, well, I'm glad. Now you can pay back the Governor of the Bank of England.'

'Indeed and hopefully put the whole sorry mess behind us.'

Just then there was a frantic knocking on the door. Sandy opened it and one of the guards was outside looking very sorry for himself.

'I'm afraid we've lost him, sir,' he said to Sandy.

'What do you mean 'lost him'?'

'I'm afraid he's dead, sir.'

'What!' Sandy shouted. 'What the hell happened?'

'We were watching him closely like the gentleman here said to do,' pointing at me, 'and he asked to go to the toilet. You know, the one in his office.'

'Yes, continue, man,' Sandy said angrily.

'Well, we didn't think anything of it so he went in and closed the door. Then, when he didn't come out, we broke the door down and found him lying dead on the floor. He must have taken some kind of poison. His lips were blue. I'm terribly sorry, sir.'

'Blue lips, eh? Obviously cyanide,' I mused.

'Oh, get out of here,' Sandy yelled 'and consider yourself suspended.'

'Yes, sir,' said the guard, saluting but looking very sorry for himself.

Sandy closed the door and collapsed into a chair. 'What a mess!' he said.

'So he fell on his sword. I should have thought of that. The gentleman's ultimate retreat from reality,' I said. Then I added, 'Well, Sandy. Look on the bright side. No embarrassing trial to go through. And, hopefully, no loose ends.'

He brightened at my words, the politician in him coming to the fore and calculating the damage. 'We can say he had a heart attack at work,' he said.

'Now you're thinking clearly,' I replied.

I left No. 10 the same way I had arrived and was soon in my car driving home to collect a few things. Then I was off back to Chequers. But I was worried. It had all been too simple. I didn't believe for a moment that Sir Edward had been acting alone. It didn't smell right. He didn't have either the ruthlessness or the knowledge to have hired the killer of the surgeon and his wife, let alone the man who had shot Pamela's attempted murderer outside the police station. There was too much apparently random mayhem. And I still wondered who wanted to see Pamela dead. It all added up to a big, fat conundrum. I knew, however, that now we just had to wait to see what, if anything, transpired.

Chapter 10
Wednesday pm

It was 12.00 by the time I got home and my cleaning lady was just leaving. I paid and thanked her, then went into my flat, threw some more clothes into a bag and a few other things I deemed to be essential in the circumstances and was ready to leave again within 10 minutes. Before I did, however, I had a couple of phone calls to make.

The first was to Sam to find out if he knew anything further. It was good to hear him, an anchor in a very uncertain world, but he had nothing more for me. They had fitted a tape recorder to the answering machine but so far no-one had called. I wondered if this was evidence of yet another mole who had access to information he shouldn't have. I said my goodbyes and rang Joe at Chequers. He said in a more excited voice than I had ever heard him use before, 'I'm glad you rang, sir.

Perhaps it would be a good idea to hasten your return here.'

'What's happened, Joe?' I asked worriedly.

'About an hour ago we had a break-in. But everything's under control now. Nothing to worry about.'

'OK, Joe. I will, as you say, hasten my return to you,' and rang off.

I drove like a maniac back to Chequers, the adrenalin flowing fast and free, and made it in record time, luckily without being stopped for speeding. When I got there, the first thing I saw was the corporal on duty with a massive bruise on his face. 'How did you get that?' I asked.

'We had a bit of a dust-up a while ago with a couple of interlopers. They were quite hard to subdue.'

'Where are they now?' I said.

'Safely trussed up in the sin bin,' he replied.

'Where's that?'

He pointed wordlessly to a small building set a little way away from the main house. As soon as he opened the gate, I drove there as fast as the gravelled driveway permitted. It was the guard house and when I went in, I found Joe looking unusually flustered. He said, 'Boy, I'm glad you're here, sir. This is a first for us.'

'Tell me what happened,' I said.

'One of the infra-red alarms was tripped and we found these two guys prowling round the house. It took four of us to subdue them. They're pretty tough and they were carrying these,' he said, pointing to two Russian Kalashnikov submachine pistols lying on a table in the small room. 'What worries me is how close they got to the house.'

'Can you take me to them?' I asked.

'Of course, sir.'

He led me down to the basement level where there were two small police-type cells. In each there was a large man, both of whom did indeed look tough. They were handcuffed and had their legs tied to hard, upright chairs. They were also gagged.

I said to Joe, 'Looks like you did a good job, Joe.' He looked pleased at the compliment and said, 'They smell like mercenaries to me.' They did to me too. I had met enough of them in Africa once upon a time.

'I need to interrogate them separately,' I said.

'I knew you would say that, sir. I think if we take them upstairs one at a time that should work.'

'That's fine, Joe.'

So a couple of armed soldiers took one of them out of his cell and hauled him upstairs after first untying his legs. There, in the main guard room, he was strapped to another chair. I pulled the tape off his mouth as gently as I could. I knew that he would be a tough nut to crack but I also knew that a little kindness goes a long way in situations like these. I had already borrowed a packet of cigarettes and a lighter from a guard and I offered one to our captive who smoked it greedily. I waited till he had finished, then said, 'You're in a pretty pickle, you know. Breaking into Chequers carries a mandatory life sentence.' I wasn't at all sure if this was true but I said it anyway. 'You might as well tell us what's going on.' No response. 'What's your name?' No response. 'Perhaps I should put you straight on a few things. I have the power to lock you up and throw away the keys forever. But, if you cooperate, I might just let you go. After all, no real harm's been done to anybody.' At last, a flicker of interest in the man's eyes.

He said in a broad South African accent, 'Are you on the level, mate?'

'You'll have to decide that by yourself,' I said.

He hesitated for a few seconds and then said, 'OK. I'll tell you as much as I know myself.' And the dam broke. 'We were told on the phone to go to a particular locker at Euston station at a particular time. We would find it open and inside would be instructions and £50,000 in cash in a holdall.' And the guns, I thought to myself. 'We went there and the speaker on the phone was kosher. Everything was there. The instructions said we had to come to this address and check it out for any signs of a woman. We weren't told that it was guarded by bleeding soldiers,' he said, looking bitterly at Joe who had been standing behind me all the time, watching the prisoner.

'Yes, I guess that must have been a bit of a shock,' I said sympathetically. 'Were you told to kill the woman if you found her?'

'No comment.'

'I'll take that as a yes if you don't mind,' I said. 'I have just one more question. This geezer who phoned you. What did he sound like?'

'He sounded posh, that's all I can tell you.'

'Would you recognise his voice if you heard it again?'

'Maybe.'

'OK. Thanks. That'll be all for now. Take him away, Joe.'

Joe disappeared with the as yet unidentified man and reappeared a few minutes later. 'Do you want to speak to the other one now?' he asked.

'No, not immediately,' I said. 'Can they communicate between their cells?'

'No. I have a man watching them and the one you managed to get talking has been re-gagged.'

'Good. Now what I would like you to do, Joe, if you can, is to find any recordings you might have of the Cabinet Secretary lying around. And then to bring them here with a recorder to play them on.'

'That should be fairly straightforward,' he said, asking no questions about my strange request. 'We have recordings of various Cabinet meetings that were held here.'

'Good man. Meanwhile, I'm going to see how Miss B. is getting on.'

We split up as we went into the main house. I went upstairs to Pamela's room and knocked. Her clear voice invited me in and I entered to find her reading a potboiler she must have been lent by one of the staff. She jumped up and said enthusiastically, 'How good to see you, Jack.'

'Good to see you too, Pamela. Safe and sound. I'm relieved. How have you been treated?'

'Like a real queen,' she laughed. 'If this is a prison, it's the most comfortable one I could imagine.'

I smiled at her and said, 'Actually, Pamela, there's a bit of a problem outside the house. I'm afraid I have to leave you again for a bit.' She looked crestfallen and I said, 'Don't worry. I'll try to be back by suppertime.'

'OK, Jack. You go and get on with your mysterious doings. I'll be fine. After all, I've got lots of nice men to look after me.'

I smiled at her again and left. Then I went to the office, rang Sandy and asked him to beef up security at Chequers. It took longer to speak to him this time but, when I got through, he agreed without asking questions. That done, I called Joe on the internal phone and asked him how the search for Sir Edward's voice was going. He said everything was ready and then I asked whether he had thought of photo-

graphing and fingerprinting the men. He
had and had already sent off the pictures
and dabs to the MOD. I suggested sending
them to MI6 and MI5 also and he agreed
that was a good idea. It would be done
immediately. I added that I was returning
straight away to the Guard house and he
said, 'We're waiting for you, sir.'

I went back outside and took a deep
breath of pure Buckinghamshire air, so
different from that of London. Then, going
back inside the guard house, I asked Joe
to play some of Sir Edward's voice to me. It
came out very clearly. He was not talking,
fortunately, about anything secret. It
was just something to do with a previous
budget.

'Fine,' I said. 'Now please bring up the
same guy again.'

He reappeared quickly with the prisoner and tied him to the same chair. I took
the tape off his mouth again.

'I could do with a drink,' he said.

'Get him a drink of water, please Joe,' I
said. When it came, he drank greedily and
then eyed me speculatively.

I said, 'I'm sure your identity is on file
somewhere. We will know your name soon.
If you continue to cooperate, I will have you
deported back to South Africa and there

will be no further repercussions for you. Do you understand?' He nodded, then I said, 'I want you to listen to a recording carefully and then tell me if it's the same man who phoned you.' He nodded again and I played about a minute's worth of the recording to him. He concentrated and, when I switched it off, said with absolute conviction, 'No, it's not the same man.'

My heart sank as my worst fears were realised and I knew that the conspiracy went much deeper and wider than just Sir Edward.

Chapter 11
Wednesday pm (cont.)

I knew I had to go through the motions and interview the other man but I also knew in my gut that the story wouldn't change. I believed that what the first guy had said was the truth, at least as far as he saw it. Joe came in during my unhappy musings and said, 'We know who they are now.'

'Good,' I said. 'So tell me.'

'A couple of South African mercenaries, as we suspected, who must have entered the country on false passports. They are both on the black list and MI6 are very keen to interview them. The one you spoke to is called Hans Eiger and the other is Christian Barnard.'

'Well done, Joe. We make slow but steady progress.'

'Somebody must have gone to a lot of trouble to get them into the country.'

'You're right, Joe. I'm ready for Mr Barnard now.'

'Coming right up, sir.' Joe went away and came back with another guard. They were both trying to restrain Barnard who was struggling to get free. After they had re-tied him to the chair, I took off the tape covering his mouth and went through more or less the same rigmarole as with Hans Eiger. But he just sat there, glaring at me, saying nothing. Finally I lost patience and said, 'Listen Christian Barnard, we know who you are. We also know that MI6 would dearly love to interrogate you. Your pal has already spilled the beans about the 50 grand, the instructions and the job you were sent here to do. Now why can't you be sensible and cooperate? You didn't kill anybody and I am prepared to offer you the same deal as I offered Mr Eiger, to deport you back to South Africa with all charges dropped. I can't say fairer than that.'

I knew I had finally got through to him. He lifted his head which he had lowered during my little speech and looked me in the eye.

'If you know all that, what do you need me for?' he said.

'I would just like you to confirm something your buddy said.'

'What's that then?' he asked suspiciously.

'I want you to listen to a tape and tell me if it's the same man who gave you the original instructions to go to Euston.'

'Is that all?' he asked incredulously.

'There may be a couple more small details you can help with. But, basically, that's it for the moment, yes. But first tell me, is there any chance the man's voice was disguised?'

'No, I don't think so,' he replied immediately.

'OK, Joe. Play him the tape, please.'

Joe did as I had requested and our prisoner concentrated on it. Then he said, 'No, it was a different voice. The man's voice who phoned us was deeper for one thing and had a different quality to it. But it's the same kind of accent.' Posh, I thought.

'OK, thanks. That's what I needed to know. Now can you tell me who provided you with the passports to enter the country?'

'They arrived through the post along with unsigned, typed instructions to get to England quickly and await further orders. We had no idea who sent them but there was enough money in the envelope to give us a good incentive to come.'

'OK, fair enough. One final question: After you had got rid of the woman, who were you supposed to report to?'

'We were given a phone number?'

At last, I thought, we're getting somewhere. 'Could you give it to me, please?'

He reeled off a number starting with 07, obviously a mobile, which I wrote down.

'Thank you,' I said. 'You can take him back now, Joe.'

After he had left, I sat back, thinking about my next move. When Joe returned, I said, 'Where is the most heavily guarded MOD base in the country you know of?'

'Probably our nuclear weapons base in Forsythe.'

'Is there any way they could be transported up there and kept on ice until their usefulness is over? I'm worried about their safety.'

'It's a long trip,' he said. 'But, in principle, I don't see why not.'

'You are going to be reinforced here soon. Maybe a few of the reinforcements could take them? I want to keep you here.'

'OK, sir. I'll try and set it up. Perhaps we could fly them from Northolt? That would be much quicker.'

'Fine. But I need their identities kept secret from all but your army chums, especially from MI6.'

'Understood. I'll get onto it straight away.'

'Good man. One other small thing before you start: Could you ask chef to prepare something nice for Miss B. and myself for dinner? I think I deserve a decent meal.'

'Of course, sir. It will be done.'

'Thanks again, Joe.'

'My pleasure, sir.'

I went back to the office and phoned Sandy again. I gave him a summary of everything that had happened that afternoon and he gasped, realising the implication as I knew he would. Then I gave him the phone number I had been given by Barnard and asked if it could be traced without any fuss being drawn to it.

He said, 'You know it's more difficult with a mobile, don't you, Jack?'

'Of course,' I replied impatiently. 'But it's the only lead we've got. Don't forget that somebody will have to ring it to confirm Pamela's death.'

'Why not get one of your prisoners to do it?' Sandy asked. 'They seem cooperative enough.'

I kicked myself for not thinking of that and said, 'Good idea. But we need to know where that phone is first.'

'I'll get onto it straight away, Jack,' he said, echoing Joe's words. 'By the way, those reinforcements should be arriving soon.'

'Thanks, Sandy. Ring me the moment you hear anything.' And with that I rang off.

It was time to make myself presentable for Pamela. So I went back to the car, took out my stuff and then back again to my room in the main house. There I had a long, satisfying shower and changed into some clean, comfortable clothes. By now I was very hungry and I rang down to find out the status of our dinner.

'It is ready whenever you are, sir,' the chef said, when I was put through to him.

'I can't wait,' I said. 'We'll eat in the small dining room if that's OK with you. You can expect us shortly.'

'Fine, sir,' came the cheery voice again.

I went across to Pamela's room and knocked rather diffidently, feeling like a teenager on a first date. I heard her voice say, 'Come in,' and went in to find her putting on some make-up and dressed in a fetching frock I hadn't seen before.

'Glad you're back, Jack. Problem solved?'

'Temporarily, yes. I'm starving. How about you?'

'Me too.'

'Nice frock,' I commented.

'Yes, isn't it? Wonderful Joe found it for me, along with make-up and everything else a girl could want.'

'Good. May I escort you to dinner, ma'am?'

'You may indeed, kind sir.'

We went downstairs to the small dining room, which had comfortable chairs around a normal-sized dining table, unlike the main dining room which was huge with an oppressive atmosphere. We found the chef there, lighting a candle with a bottle of what looked like expensive red wine already opened and the table laid for two.

'I hope you both like crab soup, steak and chips, and a nice meringue pie to finish with,' he said, looking at me.

'Sounds perfect to me,' I said, looking at Pamela.

'I'm afraid I chose the menu with chef,' she said gaily.

'How did you know what I like?' I asked.

'Inspired guesswork,' she said laughing.

'Back soon,' chef said.

I poured a glass of wine for both of us, after pulling out Pamela's chair for her, and swallowed mine in two gulps. It was like drinking pure velvet. 'That *is* good,' I said, looking more closely at the label on the bottle. It said 1956, a few years before I was born. Pamela sipped hers and then agreed that it was indeed very good. I felt now was a good time to apologise.

'I'm sorry I suspected you of skulduggery,' I said.

'So I'm in the clear now, am I?' she replied happily.

'Absolutely,' I confirmed.

Then the food arrived and we attacked it with gusto. It was every bit as good as the wine and we polished it all off without talking.

'Good to see a girl with a decent appetite,' I said finally.

'I'll pay for it later,' she said, laughing and patting her trim stomach.

I turned to chef, who was in the room tidying the dirty dishes and said, 'Definitely one of the best meals of my life, chef.'

'Here, here,' Pamela put in.

He beamed at the compliments and then discreetly disappeared.

I turned to Pamela and said, 'I'm afraid I might have to leave you alone again soon.'

'More derring-dos, Jack?' she smiled.

'I hope not. But I'm going to leave you with a gun this time.' I called Joe and asked him to provide Pamela with a pistol. He sounded dubious but I said that she was perfectly capable of handling a gun. He entered the room with a small but efficient revolver. She stripped the gun quickly, looked at the boring, reassembled it and tried the strength of the pull. Then she loaded it quickly with ammunition Joe had brought and put on the safety catch. Joe looked on impressed and I said, 'Don't worry, Joe. She's on the right side. She's been in the Army and it's for her own protection.'

'Were you really, ma'am?' he asked with new respect.

'As a matter of fact, I was,' she replied.

'The way you did that was straight out of the training manual,' he said.

'Satisfied, Joe?' I asked.

'Perfectly, sir.'

Then my phone rang and, knowing it had to be Sandy, I made my excuses and left them to reminisce about the good old days. Outside the room I said, 'Can you ring me back on the secure phone in the office?'

'Sure,' came Sandy's voice.

I crossed the large hall and went into the office. The phone rank almost immediately and Sandy's voice came through loud and clear.

'You were lucky,' he said. 'The phone number *is* a lead. It belongs to a certain Mr Tattershall, a solicitor in the City.'

'A solicitor,' I gasped, having expected it to be another hoodlum.

'Yes, I haven't got much information yet but he seems to be one of the unsavoury variety.'

'That's a relief,' I said ironically. 'Do we know where he is?'

'He should be at home. After all, it's 9.30 in the evening.'

I hadn't realised the time. Where had it gone? Then I remembered Pamela and the lovely meal we had just enjoyed. 'Can you bug the mobile?' I asked.

'I don't see why not. I will get my people onto it.'

'Good. Straight after the call comes through from here, I want him and his phone picked up.'

'OK. That shouldn't be a problem.'

'Let me know when everything's in place and I'll make the call. How long do you think you'll need?'

'About an hour should do it.'

I went back to the dining room but found that Pamela had already left. So I went up to her room and, after she had invited me in, she said, 'I've been cooped up in this house too long. After a meal like that I need a walk.'

I went back to my own room and retrieved my old MI5 gun, one of the essentials I had brought with me, and tucked it into my belt at the back so it was covered by my jacket. Then I left to find Pamela standing at the top of the staircase. We went down and out of the front door into the dark Buckinghamshire night.

'This is lovely, isn't it?' she said, breathing in the scent of newly-mown grass.

'We can't go far,' I said. 'There are sensors everywhere.'

'Let's just stroll around the house.'

When we were on the far side, out of earshot of any possible eavesdroppers, she turned to me and asked in a steely voice, 'How did you find out I was in the Army? It was supposed to be Top Secret.'

'I know. I asked Sir Maurice for your file.'

'So now you know everything there is to know about me?'

'No, not everything. Just a few facts about your life.'

She seemed mollified by my answer and we walked on in silence. Then she asked, 'Am I ever going to be told what's going on?'

'I'm not sure,' I admitted.

'At least you're honest,' she said.

'I like being with you,' I said impulsively.

She turned and gave me a soft kiss on the cheek. 'And I like being with you too. You make me feel all warm and secure.'

Then my mobile trilled again and I knew it was back to work. 'Please come back inside now, Pamela,' I said.

She followed me back through the front door and went on upstairs. I turned and went into the office. 'They're all set up,' I heard Sandy say.

'Good. I want to know if he dials another number straight after receiving the call and what that number is. Can you give me the number of the guy who's going to arrest Mr Tattershall?'

He gave me a number and I noted that down too. 'OK. I'll go now and get one of the prisoners ready to make the call.'

We hung up and I went back to the guard house where Joe was waiting. 'Bring me Christian,' I said. When he was in the room and secured, I asked him, 'What exactly were you supposed to say to the

guy after you had done what you came to
do?'

'Done and dusted,' he replied simply.

'If you are deceiving me, I'll have your
guts for garters,' I said, repeating Sandy's
words when all this started.

'I have no reason to do that,' he said.

'Did it matter which phone you called
on?'

'No.'

So I dialled the number Christian had
given me, passed the phone to him and
whispered, 'Don't deviate from the script.'
He took it and after a few moments it was
answered. He said the three words he was
told to say and passed the phone back to
me. I heard the sound of the connection
being broken. The prisoner was removed
and I waited a few more minutes, then
called the number Sandy had given me. I
heard a brusque voice say, 'Yes, who is it?'
I identified myself and said, 'Have you got
him? And his mobile?'

'Yes, sir.'

'Good. Now drive him somewhere totally
secure, in a tank if need be. No communi-
cation with anyone. Is that clear? I'll be
back in London tomorrow.'

'Yes, sir.'

I hung up and then asked Joe to leave the room. After he had gone, I rang Sandy again and said, 'Any news on the other number called?'

'Yes, but I'm afraid it was completely untraceable. Sorry about that, Jack.'

'Oh well, I guess I expected no less. But at least we've got the guy who made the call.'

'So, what next?'

'I'll be back in town tomorrow to interrogate our bent solicitor.'

'Good luck with that. Keep me posted.'

'Thanks and I will.' I was tired of the phone and all these shenanigans but knew there was one more thing I had to do before I went to bed. I called Joe back in and asked how the preparations for the transfer of the prisoners were going. He said that they would be in place by the next morning.

'Good,' I said. 'Get rid of them as quick as you can. I'll be off to London tomorrow. Oh, and by the way, don't go falling for any of Miss B.'s feminine wiles, will you?'

He looked shocked and said, 'Who, *me*, sir?'

After that little exchange which made me feel better, I went back to my room and collapsed into bed. I hoped that I had at least bought some time for Pamela.

Chapter 12
Thursday am

My sleep was interrupted by a lurid dream of me sitting completely naked on a cloud waving to people below but at least I felt reasonably refreshed when I got up. I did my normal morning ablutions, had breakfast alone and then set off for London at a leisurely pace, ruminating about the solicitor. Obviously he was working for others whom I knew were dangerous. But who on earth had the power to infiltrate government to the level at which they clearly had? I didn't believe in coincidences and felt that Sir Edward would not have committed suicide just because of my threats. He was even more afraid of somebody else. As, indeed, I suspected Mr Tattershall was. At that thought I quickened my pace, suddenly afraid myself.

As I approached London, my mobile rang and the same voice I had heard the evening before, the one of the policeman, said, 'Can you come straight to Wormwood Scrubs, sir?'

'Certainly,' I replied, thinking that that should be as secure as any place in Britain.

I got there at eleven by my watch and went straight through to the isolation wing where I was directed. There I found a lot of warders rushing around, looking worried. I stopped one of them and asked what was going on. In turn he asked for my ID and, when I showed it to him, asked if I was the chap 'they' were waiting for. I had no idea who 'they' were but I said yes anyway and he directed me back out of the isolation wing to the Warden's office. I was truly worried myself by now and, as I approached, I heard raised voices. I walked straight in and found a full-scale row in progress. It was between the Warden, a good chap I had met a couple of times in the past, and a Chief Super who was doing most of the shouting.

'What's going on, Harry?' I said, addressing the Warden.

'Good to see you, Jack,' he said. 'I presume you are the one ultimately responsible for Mr Tattershall?'

'Yes, that's right,' I said. 'Is he OK?'

'I'm afraid not. He's topped himself. Just a short while ago.'

'What?' I cried, aghast at this turn of events, although deep inside I was not surprised.

'It's true, sir,' said the Chief Super without introducing himself. 'I've seen the body myself.'

'How did it happen?' I asked more calmly now.

'He strung himself up to a nail on the wall using his shirt. Very embarrassing for us and the Warden here.'

'Yes, it is,' I said grimly, turning to Harry. 'I thought the prisoners in the isolation wing were continually checked against the possibility of suicide.'

'Yes, they are but they do it at regular intervals and chummy must have worked out the routine and chosen the few minutes he was left alone to do it.'

'Damn,' I said heatedly. 'Is there *any* possibility that it wasn't suicide?'

'We don't think it could have been murder, sir,' said the Chief Super. 'The prisoners were all in their cells.'

'What about one of the warders?' I asked.

It was the Warden's turn to look aghast and he immediately replied, 'No way, Jack.'

I thought again of the reach of the 'baddies', as I called them to myself, and said, 'I would like each warder on duty to be interrogated by the Chief Super here anyway.'

'Yes, Jack. So be it,' said the Warden resignedly.

The Chief Super, whose name I still didn't know but felt could be trusted, looked pleased that at least there was something he could do now. Then I turned to the Warden and said, 'I don't expect he'll find anything but I need to be on the safe side, Harry. I know how determined a man can be who's intent on committing suicide and how difficult it is to stop him. So I'm almost sure you're right about the cause of death.' He seemed mollified by my words and I left them to their respective tasks, the Chief Super to his interrogations and the Warden to clearing up the mess whenever one of his inmates died.

As soon as I was outside, I rang Sandy. 'I need to see you at once,' I said.

'And I need to see you too,' he replied grimly.

'I'll be there in about half an hour,' I said.

'OK. I'll be waiting.'

Chapter 13
Thursday pm

It was lunchtime by the time I reached the Treasury building but I thought resignedly I would have to forego the thought of food again. I rushed over to No. 10 through the tunnel and met Sandy in his private study. He was alone, looking pale and drawn, and closely scrutinising a piece of paper. He looked up when I came in and said in forced tones, 'Good to see you again, Jack.'

I collapsed into what had now become my regular armchair and asked, 'What's the problem now Sandy?'

'This is the problem,' he said waving the piece of paper. He passed it to me and I saw with horror that it was the same size and font as the original letter and was also unsigned. It read:

'Dear PM, First congratulations on saving the life of Miss Burrows. Your man, Jack, is very resourceful. And now to business. We have been following events with interest, especially the unfortunate suicide of Sir Edward. It's true that he was more afraid of us than of your threats but we are sure you have already worked that out. In addition to him of course, there is the solicitor whom you have arrested. You must be aware that we will reach him before you can interrogate him. But they are just pawns. We have other assets you cannot imagine and, also, more importantly, we still have proof of your conspiracy to use a double for the Queen in the six months after her death. And we still assert that leaking the information would seriously undermine the stability of the country you profess to love.

If you would like to meet a representative of ours, send Jack Sanderson to Westminster Cathedral at 2.00 pm and tell him to go into the second confessional on the right. He must be alone. Otherwise the meeting will be aborted and we will immediately release the information we have to the media. Yours faithfully etc.'

I sat back in my chair and said, 'Wow! This is a real bombshell. How did you receive it?'

'In the normal post at about 11.30 this morning.'

'So it would have been seen by at least one aide?'

'Yes, exactly. The circle of knowledge continues to widen. Fortunately, however, it was only seen by my private secretary and I have used the strongest threats I could dream up to keep him quiet.'

'What about the envelope it came in?'

'I sent it off to forensics straight away but I don't have many hopes there.'

I thought hard for a moment and then said, 'At least it shows that the leak here has been plugged. No other Sir Edward to drop it surreptitiously into your in-tray.'

'That's true, Jack, but what the hell do I do and what the hell do they want?'

'Well, obviously I have to go and meet this representative of theirs. And I'm going to have to get my skates on,' I said, looking at my watch.

'You said you needed to see me on the phone,' Sandy said.

'Yes, that's true. I almost forgot. Mr Tattershall apparently committed suicide just before I got in to see him.'

'Oh, no! Another dead end.'

'Not necessarily,' I said. 'If he was a solicitor, he will have kept documents somewhere recording details of any meetings and/or phone conversations he had

with the bad guys.. I suggest you ring Sam
Bullock and get him to put together the
best team he can muster, ones he can
absolutely trust, to search Tattershall's
office, home, bank safety deposit boxes and
anywhere else he might have hidden the
evidence. I believe there must have been
some kind of insurance policy, even if it
didn't work out like that for him. Solicitors
are careful people, even bent ones.'

Sandy brightened a little at my words
saying, 'Good idea, Jack. I'll get onto that
straight away.'

Then I left, telling Sandy that I would
be in touch as soon as I found anything
out. I looked at my watch again. 1.15. I
decided it would be quicker to take a taxi.
I wanted to reconnoitre the cathedral first.
Clever idea, I thought, to choose a confessional for a meet. The person I was meeting could remain completely anonymous.

I was there within 25 minutes and
walked in by the main door. I saw immediately that there was a large wedding
going on. I stuck out like a sore thumb in
my jeans, T-shirt and old leather bomber
jacket. But I sat down anyway at the back
and then knelt, pretending to pray with
the congregation. The confessionals were
placed further down the nave on left and

right. Four on each side. I saw nobody enter or leave the one I was interested in and presumed the fake priest was already inside. So at 1.59 I boldly walked past the large wedding party and into the confessional I had been instructed to enter. Just then the organ and choir burst into a loud Hallelujah chorus. I sat down on the hard chair feeling the butt of the pistol I had brought press into my spine but knowing also that I couldn't use it. I looked through the screen and saw two eyes peering at me which looked black in the gloom of the confessional. The organ and choir stopped as quickly as it had started and I heard the service resume.

Then there came a whisper to me through the screen, 'Do you want to confess your sins, young man?'

'No, not really,' I replied.

There was a chuckle and the whisper came back, 'You're a bit of a joker, aren't you, Jack Sanderson?'

'I suppose so. What do you want?'

'All in good time, Jack. Patience is a virtue, remember. We know all about you by the way. MI5 for many distinguished years followed by disgrace and forced retirement after your wife, Jenny, wasn't it, died of cancer and you started to drink. But your sins are forgiven, Jack.'

And I saw him make the sign of the cross on the other side of the screen. When he did that, I saw the flash of an unusual gold signet ring and, in spite of my horror at his extensive knowledge of me, thought, 'You might have just made your first mistake, mate.' Then he continued:

'We also know about your membership of the COBRA committee and how you are only on it because of your long friendship with the Prime Minister.'

'How the hell did you get all your information? It was all supposed to be Top, Top Secret,' I said.

'From the late, lamented Sir Edward of course. This is just to impress on you our power and long reach. Now to business. We want you to take a message to Sandy, your friend. Tell him that first we want him to scrap his ridiculous plans to block bankers' bonuses and secondly, to set in place plans publicly to win back the City's influence on the global stage since we left Europe. As he well knows, it has suffered tremendously both during and after Brexit and we think this has done irreparable damage to the country. He has one month to achieve a start on these goals. If we see no concrete progress by one month today, we will release the information we have on the double conspiracy. Is that all clear?' The whisper stopped. The accent, in spite of the quietness of the voice, was clearly upper class.

'Yes,' I mumbled, shocked at the scale of their ambitions.

'Don't bother trying to follow me,' were his parting words.

I saw him stand up then and disappear out of his little box, a big man dressed in priest's robes. I got up quickly and tried to follow but he was lost in the melee of the marriage procession which was starting to leave the church. There were too many priests around, all dressed pretty much identically. I sighed, realising the futility of my task.

I left the Cathedral the same way I had entered and looked around for a taxi. I got some strange looks from the wedding party who were all on the steps, preparing to have their photos taken. But I ignored them and ran across Victoria Street finding an empty taxi quite quickly and directed the driver back to the Treasury. When I arrived, I went through the usual ritual with the corporal on duty and was eventually free to hurry through the tunnel and into No. 10. I wondered how Sandy would react to this latest body blow.

I found him in his study alone staring morosely at a large pile of government papers, all presumably awaiting his signature. He jumped up and said simply, 'Well?'

'I suggest you sit down,' I said. He did and I gave him a brief summary of everything that had happened in the cathedral. I saw the blood drain from his face when I told him about what 'they' wanted but he let me finish.

'What the hell do I do, Jack?' he almost wailed. 'I'm between a rock and a very hard place.'

'I know,' I said, 'but at least we have a breathing space now.'

'We'll never catch them,' he said.

'The political decisions I'll leave up to you. But I think we have a few leads to follow up.'

'Can you deal with them, Jack?' he said.

'Yes, of course,' I said. 'You know me, "Never give up" is my motto.'

'Thank God I've got you,' he said. 'Can I offer you a drink?'

'No, thanks. Too much to do,' I said and left.

Chapter 14 Thursday pm (cont.)

It was now late afternoon on Thursday and I went to an empty office in No. 10 which I knew had a secure phone in it. First I rang Joe who said in answer to my questions that, yes, the prisoners had got off safely to the nuclear weapons base in Scotland and were due to arrive shortly and, yes, Miss B. was fine, if rather bored. I asked him for a name and a number I could call at the base and he gave me both. I wrote them down and asked him finally if I could have a quick word with Miss B. She came on the line and I said without thinking, 'I miss you,' and she replied 'I miss you too, Jack. Hurry back.' 'I'll do my best,' I promised and we left it at that.

Then I rang Sam Bullock who picked up and said, 'I guessed it was you, Jack. Thanks for cutting me in on the investigation.'

'That's OK, Sam. Any progress?'

'Well, it would help if they knew what they were looking for.'

'I'm not sure myself. But I'm thinking along the lines of any unusual names outside of his normal practice or large, unexplained payments into one of his bank accounts and tracing that back to who might have paid him.'

'OK. Well, that helps. Actually, we've only just finished clearing his office and his home of stuff. We're hoping his computer might hold a short-cut. He had tons of paper. It's a good thing he was divorced and lived alone. At least we didn't have to apply for a search warrant.'

'Yes, it was,' I said distractedly. 'Well, keep at it, Sam and let me know if anything turns up.'

'Will do, Jack.'

Another thing done. I had been thinking of the ring while I was on the phone and now decided to try to draw it. I had only seen it momentarily but I thought I had seen something like it before. It consisted of a kind of equilateral triangle without the base with a large V superimposed over it. Drawing is definitely not one of my talents but it was a simple enough image and I was soon reasonably satisfied. I thought I had seen it before in connection with some kind of secret society and I wondered who to send it to but couldn't immediately come up with any ideas. Then I realised that Sam would probably either know, or could find, somebody. So I rang him back and asked if I could e-mail a picture to him and if he could identify it or get it identified. I explained that it was on a signet ring. He said he would try so I took a close-up of my drawing with my mobile and sent it off as an e-mail attachment.

Then I sat back, thinking of what else I needed to do now. I looked up the name and number Joe had given me and, having identified myself, got through to a girl with a pleasant Edinburgh burr. I asked for Colonel Hawkins and, when he came on the line, asked if his two visitors had arrived. He said they were being processed as he spoke and I breathed a sigh of relief. Then I told him that some *very* bad guys were now certainly looking for them and that I wanted them guarded around the clock. He chuckled and promised me that they would be safer there than in the Tower of London. I reiterated grimly that the people after them would stop at nothing to kill them and that they seemed to have an extraordinarily long reach. He took me seriously then and reassured me that he would do all in his power to keep them safe.

'I hope to God that's enough,' I muttered and rang off, thinking that I really didn't want two more deaths on my conscience, even if they weren't exactly innocent ones.

I thought back over the conversation in the cathedral and especially about the fact that somebody must have accessed my file illegally and decided to give Sir Maurice a ring. So I dialled him at his office where I presumed him to be but his gatekeeper, a chap everyone called Bob, explained that he had taken the day off, complaining of a severe headache and was presumably at home. Sir M. had never suffered from headaches in his life but I knew who had given him one. I rang his house and spoke to his housekeeper who said that he was in his study and had asked not to be disturbed. I told her to tell him that Jack was on the line and that he would definitely want to talk to me. Then I heard a click on the line as one receiver was replaced and another picked up.

'How are you getting on, Jack?' Sir Maurice's false bonhomie was grating but I ignored it.

'Not bad, Sir M. The reason for ringing is that I think somebody bad has managed to access my MI5 file.'

'That's impossible, Jack,' he spluttered, all composure gone.

'I'm afraid it's happened,' I said. 'Who has access to my records?'

'Only myself and the chief librarian,' he said.

'I want him examined right down to his toe nails,' I said. 'But before that, you should check the log in the registry to see who else might have been sniffing around. Ring me on my mobile if anything turns up.'

'Will do,' said Sir Maurice, man of action again with all thoughts of headaches gone, and rang off.

I saw I had a text message from Sam so I rang him back.

'I know what the ring signifies. I had a case once which involved somebody with a ring just like it,' he said.

'Are you going to tell me or do I have to come over there and bash it out of you?'

'It belongs to somebody high up in the Masons,' he said.

'Thanks a lot, Sam,' I said and disconnected.

The Masons? The waters were getting murkier by the minute. But then again, maybe not. I remembered now where I had seen a similar design. On the front cover of a thriller I had read once about the Masons. What did I know about them? That they were apparently still powerful, an old boy's network stuffed with the Good and the Great in the country, including judges, police and leading business people. Business people, I mused. Who would benefit from scrapping the laws regarding bankers' bonuses? Bankers obviously! What were the politics of the Establishment? Traditionalist Conservative. The very people who didn't want us to break from Europe. They always wanted to preserve the status quo and we had been in Europe a long time before we broke away. Could there possibly be a conspiracy of high-up Masons who were also bankers, setting their own agenda for the country, partly for their own profit? It sounded very far-fetched but then everything about this mess was far-fetched. My powers of deduction stopped there and I decided to share my suspicions with nobody for the present. But how could I possibly access the Masons? It was, after all, a *secret* society.

Then I remembered the powers of Google. I switched on the computer on the desk, found the Internet Explorer icon and clicked. I typed 'Top Masons in the UK' into the search engine and quickly found an interesting, if obviously biased, article about how Freemasonry is corrupting our government and courts. It accused almost every top politician and even members of the Royal Family of being members. I also discovered that top Masons are called 'bilderburgers', a new word to me. I switched off the computer and thought that even if the article was only 10% true, it was still mind-boggling.

Then I thought of Sandy and wondered if he was a 'bilderburger' and decided that the only way to find out was to ask him. So I left the office and went back to his study where I found him in conference with the Health Secretary. 'Give us a few minutes, please, Jack,' he said so I paced up and down outside until the Secretary left and then marched in.

'I want to ask you a simple question,' I said.

'Ask away, old chap,' Sandy said.

'Are you a bilderburger?'

Sandy looked as if he had been slapped in the face. He looked at me carefully and said, 'What on earth are you on about?'

'I know I touched a nerve with my question. You obviously know what a bilderburger is.'

'Even if I was, I certainly couldn't tell *you*,' he said uncertainly.

'I'll take that as a yes if you don't mind,' I said, remembering another occasion recently when I had used the same words and thinking briefly of Pamela. 'I'm surprised but not shocked.'

'What do you want, Jack?' he asked bitterly.

'I just want a list of top bankers who are also top Masons,' I said.

'That will be very difficult, if not impossible,' he said. 'I don't even know if such a list exists.'

'Do you want to solve this problem you've got or not,' I said firmly.

'OK, Jack. I'll try.'

'I know you will, Sandy.' And I left him alone with his secrets. Surely one of my leads will come up trumps, I thought. Too many balls in the air or is it not enough, I thought as I left Downing Street. I would go back to my flat, have a decent dinner, go to bed and leave the hunting for clues to others. Which I did, having broached one of my good bottles of whisky to help me sleep.

Chapter 15 Friday

I slept well for most of the night but woke up at 5 am after the usual terrifying dream about Jenny. Knowing I wouldn't be able to go back to sleep, I brewed up a pot of coffee and had breakfast. Then I showered, changed my stale clothes and sat down in my writing chair. I knew I could be soon in danger myself and had to give myself some sort of insurance policy, as I was still convinced Tattershall had, so I started to write things down in order from my initial summons to Downing St to my latest suspicions. It took me a couple of hours but clarified my thoughts as I was hoping it would. Then I rang Sam again and asked if he was available to be seen. It was 11 am on Friday and he was at his desk as usual. 'Sure, come on over, Jack,' he said, sounding surprisingly cheery. I put the sheets of manuscript in an envelope, sealed it and wrote on the outside, 'To be opened only in the event of my death. Signed: Jack Sanderson.' Then I put on my jacket, hiding the envelope under it and left the flat.

I drove slowly over to New Scotland Yard and used my special MI5 permit, which I had been allowed to keep, to park outside. I hadn't detected any tails on the way. I went up to Sam's office and hearing his deep, lugubrious voice say, 'Come in,' when I knocked, went in to find the room full of detectives being briefed about a recent murder which had made the front pages. I sat at the back and waited for him to finish. It didn't take long and we were soon alone.

'I need to ask you something important, Sam,' I said.

'Go ahead,' he said.

'Are you a Mason?'

He looked at me curiously for a moment and then chuckled and said, 'No, Jack. I've been approached a couple of times but I don't believe in all that secret society stuff. Also it could compromise me in my job, I think.'

'Thank God for that,' I said, believing him. 'It's good to know that not *all* cops are corrupt.'

'It's a mistake to think that just because a cop's a Mason, he's necessarily corrupt,' he said.

'I'm sure you're right,' I said placatingly. 'I stand corrected. But I'm jolly pleased you're not one of them. I've got something I'd like to leave with you.' I passed him the envelope. 'Put it somewhere very safe. I believe that anybody who looks at the contents could be in grave danger.'

He looked at what I had written on the outside and said, 'Last will and testament, eh, Jack?'

'Something like that,' I admitted.

'I know you're mixed up in something dangerous. But now you're frightening me, Jack.'

'Please take it seriously,' I said, knowing that Sam had probably never been frightened in his life.

'Oh, I do, don't worry. I'll look after it for you. And I promise not to peek. A kind of insurance policy, is it?'

'Well guessed, Sam,' I said admiringly.

'Anything else I can do for you?'

'Yes, as a matter of fact, there is. Can I meet your team who are going over Tatershall's stuff?'

'No problem. They're not here though. I've lent them a disused safe house to work in.'

'Good thinking. Can I have the address?' He gave it to me and I asked him to ring them and tell them I was on the way. He said he would and I let myself out.

Then I was on the road again, still checking for tails, but even more carefully this time. I didn't want to lead any of the baddies to Tattershall's archive. The address was in North Finchley and I had to use the Satnav to find the house. It was buried inside a whole district of similar houses, totally nondescript. I went past and noticed all the curtains were drawn, as indeed was the case with every safe house I had ever been to. I had spotted nothing untoward on the journey but, to be on the safe side, I parked around the corner and walked back.

I knocked on the door and a youngish chap with glasses opened it saying, 'You must be Mr Sanderson. The boss told us you were on your way.' I agreed that was indeed who I was, showing my ID. 'Bring anyone with you?' he asked. Knowing he meant tails, I said, 'No, not as far as I could tell.' Then he let me in after giving a thumbs-up to a watcher on the top floor of the house opposite.

I went through to the dingy living room which had its lights on as the curtains were drawn. There were five men there and one woman, all of them either scanning the three computers in the room or sifting through the mounds of paper scattered all over the floor. They all looked up as I came in and I gave them a cheerful wave saying, 'Who's in charge then?' The chap who had opened the door and followed me inside said rather diffidently, 'Actually I am. My name's George. How do you do, sir?' holding out a hand. I shook it, thinking sourly not for the first time that cops and doctors seemed to be getting younger all the time. 'Call me Jack,' I said. 'Have you found anything?'

'Nothing definitive. But something rather odd came up just about an hour ago.'

'Show me.'

He took me to one of the computers and keyed in a few instructions. Old bank statements belonging to a Mr S. Tattershall started to scroll down the screen. He stopped at one dated a couple of years before and pointed. I noticed a direct debit payment of £5000 into his account. He scrolled on to the following month and there it was again: £5000 paid in on the same day of the month.

He said, 'And it's the same every month until now.'

I did a quick calculation in my head, 'So he's been paid over a hundred grand to do what exactly?'

'That's the odd thing, sir. There's no indication that he ever did *any* work for the money. No invoices, nothing.'

I rubbed my chin. 'Any idea where the money is coming from?' I asked.

'There is a number on the direct debit but it appears to be a dead end, some kind of shell company in Luxemburg.'

'Well done,' I said distractedly. 'Anything else?'

'Well, we checked his diary around the time of the first payment and found a meeting with somebody not accounted for by his usual business.'

My pulse quickened and I said, 'Can you show me?'

He took me over to a long foldable table with documents strewn all over it and picked up a large 5-year diary, the kind most business people have in their offices. Opening it at a page just over two years earlier, he pointed out an entry. It just said, 'Meeting with PS 2.00 pm in bar.' Just a couple of bare initials, nothing else.

'PS, eh,' I said. 'Found any mention of a PS anywhere else?'

'No, sir. Not yet.'

'Well, keep looking and keep up the good work.'

'Thank you, sir. We will.'

And I left. I wondered whether P.S. were the man's (or woman's) true initials or whether he had been using an alias. My intuitions inclined me to the latter view but there was still a small chance that he had used his real name. I hoped Sandy would deliver that list soon. I decided that there was not much more I could do for the present and felt I deserved some R & R after all the hectic running around of the past few days. And where better than Chequers I thought, remembering the kiss Pamela had given me. So I phoned Joe and told him I was on the way back. Then I got back in the car and headed west out of London again.

Chapter 16
Friday evening

I arrived back at Chequers at about 7 pm in good time for dinner. I went up first to Pamela's room and, after being invited in, found her reading again, a different book this time. She got up when she saw me, ran over and gave me an impulsive hug saying, 'It's so good to see you safe, Jack. I've been worried.' Rather embarrassed but pleased nonetheless, I disengaged myself and looked at her. She was as bright-eyed and bushy-tailed as ever.

'Been bearing up OK, Pamela?' I asked.

'All the better for seeing you, Jack,' she said, giving me one of her impish grins.

'How do you fancy a repeat performance of dinner? I could eat a horse.'

'I'd love that, you know I would. In spite of the fact that I'm putting on far too much weight here,' she said.

'I'll organise it. Give me about an hour.'

'OK. See you later.' And I left to return to my own room. There, I showered and changed and tarted myself up again as best I could. I had already phoned chef who sounded pleased to be asked to cater for the two of us again. I suspected he was a bit of a match-maker.

I collected Pamela at about 8, having switched off my mobile. I didn't want anything to disturb our evening. We went downstairs again to the small dining room where Chef was waiting for us with yet another old bottle of wine sitting uncorked on the table.

'What have you got for us this evening, Chef?' I asked.

'I thought a fresh Bouillabaisse, followed by lamb on the rack and finishing with Bombes Surprises,' he replied.

I flinched at the word 'Bomb' but then remembered what it was. 'Sounds lovely,' I said and Pamela agreed. The opened wine was white this time to go with the fish soup and was absolutely delightful as I knew it would be. When he had left us alone to eat, I asked Pamela, 'So what have you been up to?'

'Oh, a bit of this and a bit of that,' she replied, happily tucking into the Bouillabaisse.

'You haven't seduced any of the help, I hope?' I asked jokingly but perhaps a little anxiously too.

'Why, Mr Sanderson, I do believe you're jealous,' she said mocking me.

'Of course not,' I said irritably.

'Good.' She put her hand on mine and I swear a bolt of electricity flashed between us. I withdrew my hand and said, 'Really, I'm curious about how you've been spending your days.'

'As a gentlewoman of leisure?' she smiled.

'Yes, if you like.'

'Well, I've gone for a few walks outside, always accompanied by one of Joe's tame soldiers; as I told you, I've been eating too much of Chef's yummy food; and I've been reading a lot in my room.'

'That's it? I asked incredulously.

'Pretty much so. Oh, and I've been waiting for you to come back.'

I blushed and then asked 'What do you miss most while you are incarcerated here?'

'Probably my exercise. I'm a big jogging fan and I can't do that here.'

'I'm sorry about that but you know why, Pamela. The threat's still out there.' I was sorry to have said that as soon as it came out since I thought it would cast a pall over the meal. But, although she looked momentarily disconcerted, she soon recovered and it wasn't long before we were chatting away like old friends. The meal went by in a blur and, by the time we had finished everything Chef had brought us, including the bottle of red which went down well with the lamb, I was feeling decidedly mellow.

'A nightcap?' I asked.

'No, I don't think so,' she replied, yawning theatrically. 'I think it's time for bed.'

I realised then how tired I was too and followed her upstairs. I went into my own room, brushed my teeth and lay down on the bed. But, in spite of the tiredness, I knew I was too wired to sleep. So I got up and tapped lightly on Pamela's door. She opened it, dressed in a nightgown, and the next thing I knew we were embracing passionately. I shall draw a decent veil over the rest of that night except to say that she made love with all the passion of a tigress defending her cubs. By the time I made it back to my own room, it was very late and I was in a state of considerable bemusement (and exhaustion). But I slept very well with none of my usual dreams.

Chapter 17
Saturday am

I woke up late, feeling better than I had for years, even if I was a bit scared of meeting Pamela. I realised that I hadn't felt the same since Jenny and the thought frightened me. It was the first time I had been unfaithful to her memory since her death.

We met in the breakfast room where she looked at me shyly and then said, 'I'm not in the habit of one night stands, you know, Jack.'

'Neither am I,' I replied heatedly.

'I believe you,' and she gave me another of her soft kisses. 'But I still know almost nothing about you.'

'There's nothing much to tell,' I said, relieved at the simple way the meeting had turned out.

'Don't be ridiculous. Everybody has a history. You know mine, you've seen my file, and now I think I have a right to know yours.'

'You're right of course,' I mumbled through a mouthful of toast. I had a slurp of coffee and then, very tentatively, started to tell her about Jenny. She was the first person I had talked to on such a personal level since Jenny had died and I felt like I was exorcising a ghost. She listened attentively, not stopping my flow, and when I came to a stumbling halt, got up from her chair and gave me a kiss, this time a real lover's kiss. 'Poor you!' were her only words.

'Have you never loved and lost anybody?' I asked.

'No. I've never found anyone I could love enough. But I think I can guess how you must feel.'

'What about family?'

'I was put up for adoption when I was a baby and I never really saw eye to eye with my adopted family. Didn't you read that?'

I thought back and then remembered that I had skipped over her early years as I presumed they would have no bearing on my mission. 'No, I skipped that bit,' I said. And then added, 'Poor you too.'

She smiled and we said nothing further.

After breakfast I went up to my room and then remembered my mobile which I had switched off the night before. I had a

text from Sam reporting no further progress on the Tattershall front. And another
from Sir Maurice asking me to get back to
him on his office number at my earliest
convenience. I rang him immediately and
her said gravely, 'Very bad news, I'm afraid,
Jack. Your file's missing from Registry. I
checked the log and a page has been torn
out also. God knows how this happened.
The system's supposed to be foolproof.'

'Nothing's foolproof if you're rich
enough,' I said bitterly. 'What about the
chief librarian?'

'He's gone missing. We're looking for
him urgently.'

'Well, *if* you find him,' I said, stressing
the 'if', 'you'd better make damn sure you
keep a permanent watch on him. And don't
forget to get in touch if you do. I would like
a few words with him myself. Have you
checked his finances?'

'No, not yet. I only recently realised he
wasn't at his post when I went down to
check the log.'

'I suggest you do that. It might give you
a motive for him turning traitor,' I said,
thinking of Sir Edward.

'Will do, Jack. This is very worrying.'

'For me more than you,' I said grimly
and hung up. Then I rang Sandy and he

came on the line almost at once. 'I know what you want, Jack,' he said, 'But you'll just have to be patient. It's not something I can produce just out of thin air.'

'I can't wait too long, Sandy. *My* life's in danger now and Sir Maurice has just found a traitor at the heart of MI5. I'm rapidly running out of leads.'

'Oh, no. Not MI5 as well,' he groaned.

'I'm afraid so. So I hope you see the urgency.'

'Yes, of course. I'll spend every spare moment I have on it. But I'm sure you'll appreciate that I can't simply leave the government of the country on hold while I rush around doing your bidding.'

'You bloody well can if you don't want to see your precious conspiracy leaked,' I said brutally.

'OK. OK. I'll do my best, I promise.'

'I can't ask for more than that,' I said and hung up.

I needed to put my thinking cap on and without the distraction of Pamela just across the hall so I decided to go for a walk. I rang down to Joe and asked if I could have someone to accompany me as I wanted to walk around the estate and didn't want to set off any of the sensors. He asked if I wanted him to walk with me but I said that wasn't necessary. He said he'd ask his best man and I could meet him in the Guard House. I walked slowly over to it and met a young captain who said Joe had asked him to accompany me. He had a map with him showing the location of all the sensors.

We started walking in silence while I thought. And my thoughts were not encouraging. The baddies always seemed to be one step ahead of me. I needed to think of a way to take the fight to them. And I knew that my only slender hope were the initials P.S. and Sandy's list. If I could at least get a name, I was fairly sure I could take it from there. They had tried to blackmail Sandy through Sir Edward. What if, once I had a name, I could blackmail them back? The thought was an intriguing one.

But meanwhile I knew I had to stay alive long enough to carry out my fledgling plan. Then I came back to the present and noticed we were approaching the tree line at the edge of the estate. My butterfly mind remembered something Joe had said what seemed like ages ago. 'It's very worrying. I don't know how they got so close to the house.' Or words to that effect. Then I wondered if somebody in the guard at Chequers had been bought in exchange for a map like the one the captain was holding. My senses quickened and I found myself breathing fast. I looked more carefully at the captain.

'Where have you served?' I asked mildly.

'All over,' he replied, avoiding my eyes. Now I was almost sure something was not right and I pulled out my pistol from my waistband, pointing it directly at his chest.

'Would you mind passing me your gun?' I said, pointing with my left hand at the rifle he had slung over his shoulder. I saw fear in his eyes now and knew that my intuitions had not deceived me. Then suddenly without warning, he whipped the gun off his shoulder and swung it at me. I wasn't ready for it and the gun smashed into my wrist. I dropped my revolver and grasped my wrist in pain. Now the situation was reversed and he was covering me. I knew I had only one chance and rushed at him knocking him off balance before he could pull the trigger. We both crashed to the ground and wrestled like boys in the playground. But this was, I knew, deadly serious. He was stronger than me and fitter too and, finally, breathing hard, he was straddling me so that I couldn't move.

'I have to kill you and that wretched woman,' he hissed, dropping saliva into my face.

'Why?' I asked reasonably.

'I have my orders.'

'Who from?'

'Never you mind.' And he leant over me to pick up the gun he had dropped in the scuffle which was now lying next to him on the ground, preparatory I'm sure to shooting me. But he had obviously forgotten, or had never been told, that I had been well trained by the MI5 dirty tricks department. As he leant over, he released the pressure on me, enough to bring up my knee straight into his crotch. It was his turn to gasp in agony and he rolled off me holding his privates, his face contorted. I got up shakily, retrieved my revolver and held it against his forehead, taking off the safety catch.

'Now tell who ordered you to kill me and Miss Barrows,' I said.

'I can't,' he muttered through his pain.

'And why would that be?' I asked.

'Because I don't know. I was contacted a few days ago and told to kill you and the woman or my homosexuality would be revealed to my army mates.'

'I thought that rubbish was out-dated now,' I said.

'Don't be daft. It's still very much there. Anyway, I have a wife and family.'

'OK,' I said. 'How were you contacted?'

'By phone.'

'Could you identify the voice again?'

'Maybe. I'm not sure. I was in a state of shock throughout the call. I thought I had always been so careful about my boyfriends.'

'Was it a posh voice?'

'Now you come to mention it, yes, it was.'

He seemed to be recovering fast and I knew I was in no state to resist another attack. So I hit him just hard enough on the head with my gun to lay him out for a couple of hours. Then I picked up the map and his gun and walked unsteadily back to the Guard house. I got there without incident, found Joe and gave him sketchy details of what had happened. He was horrified to find that one of his men had turned bad but went himself with a couple of other soldiers to pick up the latest trai-tor, having been shown on the map where he should be lying.

I went upstairs, had a shower and changed my muddy clothes and then, feeling much better, although my wrist was still hurting from the original blow, went across to Pamela's room but she wasn't there. I began to panic, wondering where on earth she had got to, but then realised I was being silly. I rang down to Chef who, as usual, was there in his kitchen burrow, and asked if he'd seen Miss Burrows. He answered in his cheerful West Country voice, 'She's here helping me to make vol-au-vents.' 'That's fine,' I said, ringing off. I wondered how many sides Pamela had to her from SAS soldier to domestic help but soon gave up the speculation. I had plenty of evidence now to prove how long the reach of the baddies really was and was wondering what to do next.

I decided to go on down to the kitchen and see Pamela. She was indeed there, up to her elbows in puff pastry with her sleeves rolled up, and her face red from the heat of the oven. I thought she looked extremely desirable. I said to her, 'Are you carrying your pistol?' and she nodded, pointing to the bulge in the small of her back. 'Good,' I said.

'Any particular reason for the question?'

'Just that I discovered somebody else on the estate intent on killing us both,'

I said, trying to shock her out of her complacency.

'What?' she cried, genuinely horrified.

We were talking on the far side of the kitchen from the Chef but I noticed him watching us with interest.

'Yes, we're both on somebody's target list now,' I said quietly. 'So be *very* careful.'

'Thanks for the warning. See you later?'

'Maybe. I'm not sure. I might have to leave.'

'OK. Well, you be careful too.'

'I will,' I said and left.

I went to the office checking my text messages on the way. I had another from Sir Maurice. I rang him and he picked up, saying, 'Thanks for calling back, Jack.' I was always disconcerted when somebody recognised that it was me calling but then I was always forgetting the power of modern technology.

He continued, 'I'm afraid we found the Chief Librarian dead by his own hand.'

'I'm not very surprised,' I said, thinking another useless death. How many more were there going to be?

'What about his finances?' I asked.

'We're going through them now but nothing untoward has turned up.'

'Look for *any* kind of weakness. The people who made him do this are completely ruthless in their manipulation of others.'

'Will do, Jack. Go carefully,' and he rang off.

I thought Joe would be back by now and rang him. He was there in the guard house and said, 'We've got him in the cells. He's coming round but slowly.'

'He might have a bit of concussion,' I admitted.

'And a very large headache,' Joe said. 'Do you want to speak to him now?'

'No, I'll wait a bit. After lunch will do. If you guys can revive him as much as possible, that would be good.'

'Yes, sir.'

I was hungry again after all the excitement of the morning and rang Chef. 'Any chance of a bite to eat?'

'Sandwiches do?' came the cheerful voice.

'By all means, and a vol-au-vent or two would be nice.'

He chuckled and put the phone down. A few minutes later he appeared in the office with a large plate of sandwiches and a bottle of beer, all of which I gobbled down greedily. Feeling much better, I walked

slowly across to the Guard House, thinking of the questions I still needed to ask

Chapter 18
Saturday pm

I went in to find Joe with a few other guards still eating their lunch in morose silence. I guessed they were all thinking about the potential fate of their erstwhile colleague. I apologised for interrupting and asked Joe whether he could find the captain's service record. He disappeared and came back shortly afterwards carrying a slim file. I sat down in a corner and read it. Captain Percy Dawkins was a veteran of Afghanistan until he had been posted home for unspecified reasons. I wondered whether his homosexuality had caught up with him earlier than he had said and, looking at the photo of the young man on the front page, thought what a waste of a promising life.

When they had all finished eating, I asked whether he could be brought up now. They went out and soon reappeared, almost carrying a white-faced Captain

Dawkins. They sat him down, bound his legs to a chair and left, all except Joe who stood behind me as before.

I said, 'You know, Percy, that I have the power to have you dishonourably discharged from the Army with a serious criminal record. Alternatively, I also have the power to re-instate you with full honours, in a different division of course, and no more of this lamentable episode need ever be mentioned again.'

His eyes lit up at the prospect I held before him and a little colour came back into his cheeks.

'Really?' he asked in a hoarse, plaintive voice.

'Yes, really, but it depends on you answering a few simple questions.'

'Ask away,' he said.

'Why were you posted home from Afghanistan for a start?' I asked.

He blushed and I thought he wasn't going to answer but then in a low voice he said, 'I think you know why.'

'OK,' I said. 'Fair enough. Bad for morale, eh?'

He blushed again and didn't reply. I didn't want to rub it in so continued quickly, 'Moving on, who were you supposed to report to after you had completed your orders?'

He hesitated, then said, 'I was given a phone number.'

My heart leapt but I kept my voice steady as I asked, 'What was it, please?'

He reeled off a London number starting with 02. I asked him to repeat it and wrote it down in my notebook. Not a mobile number this time, I thought excitedly. Easy to trace.

'OK, thanks,' I said. 'That will be all for now.'

Joe called the guards back and they took the captain down to the cells again. I told him to feed and water him but, above all, to watch him 24/7.

'Yes, sir,' he said, probably wondering why I was so concerned. I didn't tell him about the possibility of yet another suicide.

I went back to the office in the main house and rang Sam. When he picked up, I said, 'Can you trace a number for me, please? I want an address and a name.' He grunted assent and I gave him the number. 'I'll be waiting by the phone,' I said. I sat in the hard chair and thought about the possibility of getting closer to the core of this spider's web. I didn't have to wait long. Sam rang back and said, 'It belongs to a

Mrs Bedford of 18 Church Lane, Muswell Hill.'

'Anything known about her?' I asked.

'No, nothing. She's not on any of our files.'

I said my thanks and we rang off. It didn't sound like the core of my spider's web, certainly not the kind of address I would expect a bilderburger to live in. Far too ordinary. But then appearances can be deceptive, as I knew nearly to my cost after my affray with the captain.

I decided to return to London and see the place for myself. But first I went up to see Pamela.

She greeted me with her usual enthusiasm and I thought wryly that *I* was the one to have fallen for her feminine wiles. I told her I had to leave again and she held me at arm's length and looked deep into my eyes. 'Do promise me you'll be careful,' she said. 'I will,' I replied. 'After all, I've got something to come back to now.' She smiled and we kissed. I wondered whether I was falling in love but put the thought aside for examination later. I didn't want it to cloud my judgement. My parting words were, 'Don't forget to carry your pistol at all times or lock your door at night. I'll be back as soon as I can.' 'Yes, sir,' she said, giving me a smart military salute. It was my turn to smile and then I left.

I looked at my watch as I went to the car. It was 3.30. I wouldn't get to London until at least 5.30. Then I remembered my own danger and had an idea. I called Joe and told him I had to go up to London and did he have a car I could borrow, something not as flashy as my Merc? 'I'm sure I can rustle something up, sir,' he said, realising why I had asked. 'Can you come to the Guard House? It'll be waiting outside.' 'Thanks, Joe. You're a treasure.' I could feel his beam down the telephone line.

So I walked slowly over to the Guard House and waiting for me outside was a beaten-up old Volvo. Joe was standing next to it, holding the keys in his hand. He said, 'It belongs to one of my mates. It's his pride and joy but, when I told him it was for you, he lent it readily enough. It's been well maintained and has a new engine in it. It should do the business.'

'Thanks again, Joe. Tell your mate I'll look after it as though it were my own and bring it back in one piece.'

'I hope so, sir. I don't want to lose another friend,' and I caught a fleeting look of dismay cross his face as he remembered his erstwhile 'best man', the captain. I clapped him on the shoulder, got in and switched on the engine. It purred like a thoroughbred and I reckoned it should certainly 'do the business'. I checked the fuel indicator. It showed Full. Good. I didn't want to be stopped by anybody at an anonymous service station.

I waved goodbye to Joe and left the estate driving carefully until I got the feel of the car. It drove beautifully and I made good time on the motorway. Approaching London, I decided to go back to my flat for the night and go out to the house in Muswell Hill the next morning. But then I remembered that the baddies had my file and therefore knew my address. That was annoying as there were a few things I needed from the flat. But I thought I might know a way around that problem.

So I checked in at a large anonymous hotel on Kensington Road. From there I rang my trusty cleaning lady and said, 'Hello, Betty. How are you?'

'Fine, thank you, sir.'

'Good. I was wondering if you could do me a favour.'

'Anything I can do to help, sir.'

'Thanks. If you could go to my flat tomorrow morning and retrieve the black leather wallet I keep on top of my wardrobe, that would be most useful. Then I'd like you to bring it here if possible. Here's the address.' And I gave it to her off the hotel stationery. 'You see, I don't want anyone to know I'm back in London.'

Betty loved intrigue – she had no idea what I used to do for a living – and I knew she would do my bidding without hesitation.

'It will be my pleasure, sir. I'll be there about 10 if that's OK with you.'

'That'll do very nicely, thanks, Betty.' Another problem solved.

I knew there wasn't much else I could do that night so I went down to the hotel restaurant and had a lonely, but actually not bad, dinner. Then I went back up to my room and crashed out with half a bottle of whisky I had bought from an off-licence round the corner. I was pretty sure nobody knew I was in London. I hadn't been tailed from Chequers, I was sure of that, but I still slept with the door double-locked and my pistol under my pillow.

Chapter 19
Sunday am

I slept well, considering all the problems I was surrounded by, and woke at 7, realising I had been on the road for nearly a week and had again needed a decent night's sleep. I showered, shaved and pampered myself, putting on a new suit given to me by Joe which, not surprisingly, fitted perfectly. Then, feeling like the successful businessman I wasn't, I went down to the restaurant again and had a proper English breakfast. I paid the bill by credit card, figuring that the baddies, even if they were on my trail and knew my card number, wouldn't have time to catch up with me that way. I wasn't planning on hanging around. Then I got the car out of the basement garage and parked it more or less in front of the hotel with my MI5 disabled permit on it which I knew would deter clampers for a while. It was now 9.45 and I sat back and waited for Betty.

She appeared promptly at 9.55 and I took the document wallet off her which had a lock on it so I knew she hadn't peeked even if she had been tempted. I thanked her profusely and offered her a tenner for her trouble but she resolutely refused it as I knew she would. She was another real treasure, was Betty.

Then I pulled out into the traffic heading north. I had already checked out the address on my A – Z as the car didn't have its own Sat Nav. My way up to Muswell Hill was clear and I arrived at 10.45 outside the lady's house. I drove past slowly looking for any signs of watchers. I knew that Sam would have been tempted to put someone in place but saw nothing untoward. I parked around the corner as I didn't want her to see the old Volvo. Then I got the document wallet from the glove compartment and chose one of the many identities I had squirreled away over the years. I had decided I was to be a tax inspector, a sufficiently intimidating role that I was sure she would respect.

I walked back and knocked on the door. It wasn't the lady I was expecting who answered but a young, fit-looking man in jeans and an old but clean T-shirt.

'Who are you?' he demanded.

I showed him my ID and said, 'There have been a few seeming irregularities in the lady of the house's tax returns and I was wanting to have a quick word with her to clear them up.'

He wasn't intimidated by my ID and said simply, 'On Sunday. I don't believe you. There's no lady here. Now clear off,' and slammed the door in my face. His accent was classless London and I reckoned he must have had an education – he didn't look or sound like a manual labourer. I decided to have another go, putting on more pressure this time. I knocked again and then again until he came to the door.

'I thought I told you to clear off.'

'Only doing my job, sir. And as for working on Sunday, you should know that us tax inspectors work 24 / 7 if we have to. It says on our records that this house belongs to a Mrs Bedford. Is that right?'

He looked confused for a moment but then said, 'Oh, you must mean the old lady who used to live here.'

'Do I, sir?'

'We bought the house from her recently.'

'Oh really? There is, as far as I'm aware, no record of the transaction.'

He looked guilty for a moment and I wondered whether he'd had theatrical training like Pamela.

'No, there wouldn't be. We paid cash. That was what she insisted on,' he said.

Curiouser and curiouser. But then in my role as Tax Inspector, I asked the obvious question, 'And where did this cash come from? Houses in this part of London don't come cheap.'

That pulled him up short and he looked as if he wasn't going to reply. I nudged him by pointing out that I had wide powers to come in and search the property if I deemed it necessary. The Tax Service always recovered its money. He looked alarmed now which was where I wanted him.

'Do you have a name, sir' I enquired mildly.

'Mickey Mouse,' he retorted and seemed about to slam the door again. But I stuck a foot in it and peered round it to see crates of equipment piled everywhere. What sort of equipment I had no idea.

'I'll be back with the Police very soon,' I said sternly.

'You haven't the power,' he said uncertainly.

I went outside and immediately called Sam, who, as I'd thought, was in his office in spite of it being Sunday, and told him I was outside the house in Muswell Hill and needed reinforcements, preferably a SWAT team, asap for a search of the property. I also asked for a tap to be put on the phone at once. While the police were getting their act together, I stood watch outside the house to make sure nobody did a runner. The first lot arrived about ten minutes later and reported to me. I told them I had a suspect in the house, maybe even a murder suspect, for I had no idea what had happened to the lady of the house. Some of them went round the back and the rest stayed with me at the front. I saw the chap I had been talking to peering anxiously through a gap in the curtains and hoped he was well and truly scared and wouldn't put up a fight. I remembered that he had said, '*We* paid cash,' and wondered who he was in cahoots with. Then Sam rang and said the rest of the SWAT team would arrive in minutes and I asked whether he had had any luck with the phone tap. He said, 'No, sorry. You do get around, don't you, Jack?' 'I lead a busy life,' I replied. I thanked him for the SWAT team and turned back to its leader saying, 'I need all mobile phones in the house. Is that clear?' I was sure they had been phoning their superiors and it was them I was after. 'Yes, sir,' he said. Then the rest of the team arrived and were given their orders, half of them going around the back.

I walked up to the door again and knocked hard. No response. I backed away from it and nodded to the field commander. He gave the order to enter the property and then all hell broke loose. As they battered down the doors, I heard shots coming from the back of the house and a voice inside shouting, 'Don't come any closer! We have a hostage and the place is wired!' I turned to the commander who was listening on his radio. 'The shots were fired from inside the house,' he said.

'Anybody hurt?'

'One guy took a round in his flak jacket but he's fine.'

'Damn!' I thought. This was exactly the situation I had been hoping to avoid, a worst-case scenario. But I couldn't hold up my investigation for a couple of terrorists, however well educated they were. The police needed a negotiator. I needed to get inside. 'Do you have stun grenades with you?' I asked. 'Yes,' came the short reply.

'I want you to go in using every method at your disposal, short of ultimate force.'

The commander looked dubious and said, 'That goes against every rule in the book in a hostage situation.'

I said, 'I know. But I think they're bluffing. Are you prepared to give it a go or do I have to get Commander Bullock to give the orders?' I was praying I was right about the bluff.

He saluted smartly, if rather reluctantly, and said, 'Yes, sir. We'll give it a go.' He gave the orders and I saw the entire contingent tense up, all of them thinking of the disaster that would ensue if there was a civilian in there and he or she got hurt.

Then there was an awful lot of noise and confusion and I ducked behind a car, remembering Pamela's admonition to be careful. I wondered what the neighbours behind the police cordon in this respectable area were making of it all. However, it was all over quite quickly and I saw the team leading two men out in handcuffs looking dazed, one of them the man I had spoken to earlier. 'The house is empty, sir. It's not wired,' one of them reported and the Commander told his team to stand down.

'Did you get their mobiles?' I asked.

'One of them,' the policeman replied. 'The other had been smashed to bits.' The one used to phone their superiors, I thought bitterly.

'What about the equipment I saw in the house?'

'It was a bunch of computer stuff, high end by the looks of it. Most of it hadn't even been opened.'

'Is it safe for me to go in?' I asked the leader.

'I'd wait a few minutes for the smoke to clear, sir. By the way, how did you know they were bluffing about a hostage?'

'It was just a hunch,' I admitted, thinking about the man who had opened the door to me. He hadn't looked the hostage-taking type.

'Well, it was a good one,' the Commander said with grudging respect.

'Where are you taking the men?' I asked.

'To the local nick to be charged. Then they'll be remanded in custody. I don't know where.'

'I need them watched 24/7 and I want to be in on the preliminary interrogation,' I said. 'Can you find out their names?'

'We'll do our best, sir.'

'And get a team to go over the house with a fine tooth comb. I want to know what they were doing.'

'They're already on their way, sir.'

'Thanks for all your help, Commander. I'll wait here for them. Oh, and can I have the mobile phone you collected?'

'I'm afraid that's evidence, sir.'

More delay, I thought, when I really haven't got the time. 'Yes, of course. Sorry,' I said.

I rang Sam Bullock again and gave him an up-date. He said, 'Computer stuff, eh? Cyber-terrorists?'

'Could be,' I said, 'but they are connected somehow with this case I'm working on. Listen, Sam. I need to know all the numbers stored on that mobile the police have got.'

'A bit tricky that. I can't tamper with evidence.'

'It's important, Sam.'

'OK. I'll do my best.' I thanked him and before I rang off, I told him to let me know where the prisoners were being held.

Then I went through the smashed door and into the house. Architecturally, it was similar to a million others in the London suburbs but I wasn't interested in the architecture. I was, however, *very* interested in the plans taped to the living room walls. They were mostly plans of computer schematics, meaningless to me, but one caught my eye. It had a kind of family tree on it with a bunch of initials forming the names. The one at the very top said, 'S. R.'. Sandy Richards, the PM, I wondered. Further down was one which said, 'E. P.' That one had a line drawn through it. Sir Edward Petrie? I thought I recognised some of the other initials too and stuffed the plan in my pocket to prevent it being taken away as evidence too. There was nothing else of obvious interest to me in the house and I went outside to clear my head of the smoke fumes. Just then the forensics team arrived and went on in, eyeing me suspiciously. I showed their leader my ID and he asked if I had touched anything.

'Nothing,' I said, all innocence, 'I just went in for a quick shufti. I'd be interested, however, in being told what those computer plans on the living room walls mean.'

'All in good time, sir,' he said with a policeman's indifference to haste.

'Well, I'll be off then,' I said. We shook hands and I left.

I knew I had to show Sandy what I had found so I drove back to the Treasury, parked, went through the usual routine and emerged inside No. 10. I found an aide who took me to Sandy. This time he was in the Cabinet room surrounded by a number of his close political colleagues. I apologised for interrupting and told the meeting that I had to speak to the PM on a matter of some urgency. Sandy asked for the meeting to be adjourned for twenty minutes and I followed him up to his private study. He said on the way that they had been trying to find a successor for Sir Edward.

Once inside he immediately said, 'Not more bad news I hope, Jack?'

'Not exactly but I found something in a house occupied by a couple somehow connected with all this which I think you ought to see.' And I pulled out of my pocket the by now rather crumpled family tree, passing it to him.

He looked at it swiftly and said, 'So what?'

'Look more carefully at the initials, Sandy.'

He did and then gasped, 'It's my cabinet and closest advisors.'

'I thought it might be and I think the baddies might be trying to penetrate No.

10 again, this time by hacking into your computers.'

'Can they do that?'

'Nothing is impossible if you have the right gear, a few passwords and the expertise.'

'But where would they have got the passwords?'

'From Sir Edward, I suspect, as part of the deal with him. I think I interrupted the plan before it came to fruition but it might be wise to change all the passwords just to be on the safe side.'

'OK, Jack. It will be done. Anything else?'

'Yes, I want to see that list I asked you for.'

He blanched but recovered, put his hand in his pocket and withdrew a single sheet of paper saying, 'I'm breaking some of the most serious oaths I have ever made by giving you this, you know.'

I nodded and held out my hand for the paper, skimming quickly down the short list of names on it written in Sandy's own handwriting. No P. S. Damn! I had been so sure I had been on the right track. But I was still convinced that there was a Masonic connection somewhere.

He said, 'It's incomplete, I'm afraid. But it's all I could get in the time I had. Also those guys are all London-based. I have no control over names in the Provinces.'

'London-based is fine,' I said, believing the conspiracy had to be based there. 'What do you mean 'incomplete'? Are there any other bilderburgers you haven't included on the list?'

'Yes, a few. But I'm not sure if they have any connection to banking.'

'Tell me their names please.'

Reluctantly he wrote a few more names down for me. And there it was. Sir Paul Smythe!

'What do you know about this guy?' I asked, pointing to the name.

'Not much, I'm afraid. He was made a bilderburger before my time. He's reputed to be very rich and a big donor to charity. He's also very reclusive. And that's about it. I've never actually met him.'

I could have hugged him in my excitement but I didn't show it.

'Thanks, Sandy. That may be some help.' And I left, retracing my steps out of No. 10. Once outside I rang Sam and asked where the two guys his men had arrested were now. He told me the address of the police station in Crouch End near

Muswell Hill and I asked if it would be OK to go there now. He said he'd set it up and I thanked him and rang off.

I drove up to Crouch End thinking about this new development and knew I had to see Sir Maurice again to access his computer. But that could wait a while longer. First I needed to interrogate the two prisoners.

I stopped at a café and had a bite to eat, determined not to miss lunch again. Then I arrived at the police station and, having shown my ID card to the sergeant on duty, was directed down the hall to an office. I was summoned inside by an oldish barrel-chested cop with a Chief Superintendant's braids on his shoulders. He looked tough and efficient. I introduced myself and he said, 'We've been waiting for you. They've been charged with possessing an illegal weapon, attempted murder of a police officer and a whole bunch of other stuff, enough to put them away for a nice long time. We know who the older chap is, a professional minder from North London. He's on our books already but the younger man is off our radar. He's refused to say anything.'

'I'd like to speak just to the young chap if I may?' I said.

'By all means. Hope you don't mind if somebody sits in with you?'

It wasn't what I wanted but I knew I couldn't say no. So I just said, 'That'll be fine.'

He took me to an interview room with the usual two-way mirror in it. I knew I'd have an audience anyway but I'd have to be very circumspect in my choice of words. I waited there for a few minutes, then the prisoner was brought in, accompanied by another police officer who stationed himself in the corner.

'Hope they're treating you well?' I asked affably.

No reply. Just a glare.

'I told you I had the power to bring the police but you didn't believe me, did you?'

Another glare.

'Perhaps I should also tell you that I have the power to lock you up and throw away the keys. You will die in prison. You know that, don't you?'

The glare more uncertain now. He looked as if he might cry.

'Alternatively, if you cooperate, I also have the power to return you to whatever legal profession you were involved in, computers would be my guess, before you got mixed up in all this nonsense. And no harm done.'

Hope sparked in his eyes and he said, 'Immunity, do you mean?'

'That's exactly what I mean, yes. As long as you keep your nose clean in future of course.'

'And you will protect me?'

'To the best of my ability, yes.'

'I'd like to see it in writing.'

'You will but first, as a gesture of goodwill, I'd like to ask you a couple of questions.'

'Fire away,' he said eagerly, the prospect of freedom beckoning.

'What happened to the lady of the house?'

'I was told that she had been offered an extended holiday in Madeira and a substantial payment for letting us use her house.'

'Thank you. So no dead bodies buried in the garden?'

He looked shocked and said, 'No, not as far as I know.'

'Good. And my second question: Who paid for your services and for all the stuff we found in the house?'

'I don't know. And that's God's truth. I was sent an envelope containing a lot of cash. As I was broke at the time, I put it in my bank account thinking that heaven was finally smiling on me and then, a couple of days later, I received an unsigned letter saying that the money was not a gift but money for services to be rendered. I was told to come to that address where I would find schematics and an interesting problem to solve in my field. I accepted the challenge and here I am,' he said bitterly. 'We didn't even have time to unpack everything.'

'The letter was typed, I presume?'

'Yes, that's right.'

'Do you still have it?'

'No, I was told to burn it and I did.'

'OK. Thanks a lot. What's your name by the way? I'll need it for the immunity papers.' A long pause. I said, 'I think that if we trawl through the University of London's computer department's records, we'll find it easily, don't you?'

From the look on his face I knew I'd guessed right.

'Daniel Reese,' he whispered.

'Well, thanks again, Daniel. I hope you continue to cooperate with the police as you've done with me. Don't worry. I'll organise the letter of immunity.'

'You know it wasn't my gun and I didn't fire it, don't you?'

'Yes, of course.' I said although I had no idea if the police had discovered that yet. 'And that will definitely go in your favour. I can't of course promise immunity to your colleague as well.'

'Let him rot in hell,' he said, uncharitably to my mind but I let it go. 'He was a monster.'

With that I left the room and was met outside by the Chief Super who said, 'I presume you were bluffing when you talked about immunity.'

'Never been more serious in my life. I believe he's just a young man who's been led astray by money and the promise of a challenge.'

'Well, you did a good job in there anyway,' he said grudgingly.

'If you can squeeze the minder and get an identity for the sponsor, I'd be grateful. But I don't hold out much hope there. Oh, and if you can find the meaning of the schematics from Daniel, that would be good too. Relay anything through Sam Bullock.'

'Will do,' he said and we parted.

I knew my next port of call should be Sir Maurice but I gave in to the temptation to call Pamela. I just wanted to hear her voice. I was put through to her by Joe who told me that everything was fine there. I asked her how she was.

'Bored and missing you. Any idea when you'll be back?'

'Tomorrow morning if I'm lucky.'

'Try and make it then.'

'I will, I promise,' and I broke the connection.

Now it was time to pay that visit to Sir Maurice and I drove as fast as I dared down to his house in Kent. I knew his weekends were sacred unless there was an urgent flap on which demanded his presence in London and that he should be at home as he could work there just as easily as in his office. When I arrived, I had to announce myself and show my ID at the gate as usual. I was shown into the house by a tall foreign girl who introduced herself as a maid. She went into the master's sanctum and I heard voices. Then Sir Maurice himself appeared, beaming and apparently happy to see me. I asked whether we could retreat into his private study and he waved me in and shut the door.

We sat down and I said bluntly, 'I need to use your computer again.'

'By all means,' he said. 'Looking for anything in particular?' Fishing as usual. He couldn't break the habit.

'I just want you to provide me with full access if you please,' I said.

'Yes, of course,' he said, rather grumpily I thought. 'A drink before you start?'

'No thanks. I'm afraid I don't have time.'

'OK.' He went over to the computer, powered it up and typed in keystrokes as he had before, his passwords presumably. 'There you go,' he said. 'If you type a name in here,' pointing at a box in the centre of the screen, 'everything we have on him or her should be displayed.' Then he left the room.

I typed in Sir Paul Smythe and pushed the Enter button. A number of files were displayed and I started reading eagerly. That he was of interest to MI5 was immediately apparent. Why, I wondered, skipping his youth except to read that he'd been to a decent Public School, and moving straight on to adulthood. Interestingly, he was unmarried and had no children although his name had been connected with a number of socialites at one time or another. Was he gay, I wondered?

Apparently he had inherited quite a bit from his Dad but had added to this substantially when quite young from property speculation. Since then, however, his affairs had become very murky indeed. It was obvious that MI5 considered him a threat but what kind of threat was not immediately clear. His legitimate activities included being on the Boards of two well-known banks in the City, which, assuming I had the right guy, presumably accounted for his interest in seeing it prosper – nice, little earners in themselves, I thought bitterly - and giving considerable amounts to charity, as Sandy had mentioned, which accounted for his Knighthood. As Sandy had also said, he was rarely seen in public and then only at the very poshest charity galas so there were very few up-to-date photos of him in the file and the ones that were there had obviously been taken surreptitiously. I made a note of his current address and phone number and carried on reading. I also decided then to make notes on all the charities he gave to.

Then, much like I had with Pamela, I stumbled across a hidden file marked A level access only, which I knew meant only for Sir Maurice's eyes. And there it was. MI5 had decided he was threat to the country because he had secretly given large sums over the years to some *very* unsavoury criminal types, who were involved in everything from gun running to drugs to prostitution, financing their operations in return for a slice of the profits. In fact, he seemed to be a financial kingpin in all the most illegal areas imaginable although he did at least seem not to be involved in terrorism – within Britain anyway. I realised how useful it must be for him to have strong banking connections as they would have afforded him the opportunity to launder his ill-gotten gains much more efficiently.

The facts were there in black and white but there was absolutely no *proof* that he had a connection with any of these nefarious activities. It was all surmise and conjecture, circumstantial. So no hard evidence with which to charge him, I thought. A slippery customer who covered his tracks well.

I was sure now he was my man and decided that I had to have a copy of everything in the files as I hadn't had time to read the lot so I printed everything out on Sir Maurice's printer. It was a lot of paper but I thought I needed to study it all in more detail. Finally it was done and I went into the living room, having found a large empty box file into which I stuffed all the papers. Sir Maurice was there and he eyed the file suspiciously.

'Taking stuff away, are you?' he asked.

'It's for the good of the country,' I said, echoing his own words from a few days earlier.

He grinned at the reference and said, 'OK, but look after it well, won't you?'

'Don't worry. I will.' I said and with that I took my leave.

Chapter 20
Sunday evening

I knew what I had to do next and for that I had to be in London, not rural Kent. So I drove back thinking about the elusive Sir Paul. Yet another 'Sir', I thought to myself bitterly. I would be quite happy never to encounter another of those again. But I knew I had to deal with him before he wrecked even more people's lives.

When I got to London, I photocopied the papers at a business which specialised in that area and which was open on Sundays. Having done that, I put the photocopies in two large manila envelopes given to me by a helpful assistant who had left me alone to do the job, keeping the original printed-out version in Sir M.'s big box file. Then I paid and went outside laden with paper. There I phoned Sam but was told he had gone home. Of course. It was Sunday evening and I had forgotten that he must have some kind of home life.

I asked for his PA and fortunately he was there. 'Can you give me his home phone number?' I asked after identifying myself.

'It's very irregular, sir,' he grumbled.

'I know but this is urgent.'

'I can give you his mobile number,' the PA grudgingly conceded.

'That's OK. I've got it already,' I said, hanging up. I phoned the number and Sam answered. 'Glad I got you, Sam. Sorry to interrupt your weekend,' I said.

'What can I do for you now?' Sam sighed.

'I've got two packets of documents I'd like to courier over to you. I want you to look after them very carefully and put them wherever you put my 'last will and testament' as you called it.'

'No problem, Jack. I've got family here but can easily make my excuses.'

'That's great, Sam. Thanks a lot. It *is* important. Otherwise I wouldn't ask. Where shall the courier deliver them?'

'I'll have to go back to Scotland Yard. Are you in London?'

'Just about,' I said, looking at the industrial wilderness I was surrounded by.

'It'll take me about forty minutes to get into work. Do you think the courier will make it before me?'

'I seriously doubt it,' I said.

'Tell him to wait for me if I'm not there for any reason.'

'Will do. It'll be marked For Your Eyes Only. And thanks again. Will it be OK if I ring you later on your mobile?'

'It would be better if I rang you.'

'OK. Fine. Speak later. Bye.' And I hung up. I knew I still needed to ask him about whether he had managed to get any interesting numbers off the mobile that had been confiscated earlier but I didn't want to load too much on his plate at one time. Then I rang a reliable courier company I had used before and told them that I was coming by their office for them to deliver some papers for me.

'Always happy to oblige, sir,' came the cheerful voice of the dispatcher. I drove fast back to Southall where the couriers were situated. Having parked outside, I wrote 'Sam Bullock, New Scotland Yard. To be delivered into his hands only' on the outside of each of the two envelopes I'd got from the photocopying company. Then, making sure they were well sealed, I went in, gave them their instructions and paid, knowing that they would be quick and efficient.

After doing all that, I left and went back to the car. I filled up at a small service station and went looking for a suitable hotel. I found just the thing in Bloomsbury, an anonymous building near the British Museum, and registered. I lay down in my room, tired but not sleepy, and was interrupted in my thoughts by the trilling of my mobile.

It was Sam. I said, 'Everything go OK?'

'Like clockwork.'

'Good. I'm glad to have some sort of insurance policy against catastrophe.'

'If you're happy, I'm happy, Jack.'

'By the way, Sam, did you get any numbers off that mobile?'

'Funny you should ask that. I'm sitting at my desk and looking at a report on it now. There are quite a few numbers on it but only one which could hold any interest for you. The others are all lap-dancing clubs and places like that where the minder obviously hangs out. Unfortunately the interesting one is untraceable. The experts can't quite figure out why. The number doesn't answer when they dialled it. Here it is,' and he read me what sounded like a landline number starting with a prefix I didn't recognise.

'What's the prefix to?'

'Some isolated part of Gloucestershire apparently.'

'Good work, Sam. That's exactly what I needed,' I said, thinking of Smythe's address in Gloucestershire.

'I don't see that it really helps.'

'Oh, it does indeed. It's all starting to come together.'

'I'm glad. Anything else I can do to help?'

'Not at the moment but I'm sure I'll be getting back to you soon.' We said our goodbyes and hung up.

Then I went down to the small hotel restaurant and had a reasonable dinner but no alcohol. I needed to keep a clear head. I spent the next few hours reading all the papers on Smythe again until a picture of the man started to emerge. He seemed to be entirely motivated by money and self-interest. I wondered how I could get close to him and, by the time I fell asleep, I had some sort of plan.

Chapter 21
Monday am

I woke feeling refreshed and knew it was partly down to the fact that I had had no alcohol the night before. I showered, shaved, had a quick breakfast and was on the road by 9 am. Before I left, I made sure my precious box of Smythe documents was safely stowed at the bottom of my case. I was going back to see Sandy or, to be precise, his wife, Sarah. I let myself into No. 10, having gone through the usual screening process, but was told that they were out for a while. I decided to wait and think things through again. My plan certainly wasn't foolproof but I hoped it might suffice.

They got back at about 10.30 and I immediately cornered Sandy and asked if I could speak to Sarah. I had known her for almost as long as I had known Sandy and he at once gave his permission when I told him it was to do with the ongoing 'operation' but he warned me against involving her. I reassured him and once I had Sarah alone in her private quarters, we exchanged our little bits of news and the usual pleasantries before I got down to business. First I asked her if she was still a patron of Cancer Relief. When she said yes, I then asked if they had a big charity gala coming up soon. She consulted her diary and then said, 'Funnily enough, there's one coming up on Wednesday this week.' I breathed a sigh of relief and asked if she would be going. She said, 'Yes, but without Sandy. You know how charity bashes bore him. He doesn't mind donating money but prefers to keep that side of him to himself.'

I sympathised with Sandy. 'Would you mind getting me a list of the attendees, please?' I asked.

'No, I suppose not. I'll ring you tomorrow if that's OK.'

'No chance of doing it today, is there?'

'What's the hurry, Jack?'

I thought that she deserved a little of the truth and said, 'There's a guy who may be going who I very much want to talk to.'

'OK, OK,' she replied. 'I suppose that means that, if he *is* going, you will need a ticket.' She had always caught on quickly.

'Exactly, Sarah.'

'Well, you can have Sandy's. We are always invited as a pair even if he never goes.'

'That would be brilliant. Thanks, Sarah.'

'But it all depends on this guy being there, right?'

I hoped she wasn't going to give me the third degree and simply said, 'Yes.'

'And you can't tell me his name?'

'No, sorry. It's better if I keep it to myself.'

'You're still in the spying game, aren't you, Jack?'

'Yes,' I said again. 'Can you do this for me, Sarah? I don't want to get down on bended knee.'

'I'll try,' she said and fished out an address book from a bureau drawer. She dialled a number and said, 'Can I speak to George, please? It's Sarah.' A muffled response. Then another voice and Sarah asked, 'Can you do me a favour, George? I need a list of attendees at the Wednesday bash. Do you have it there?' Another response. Then, 'Thanks, George. I owe you one. Can you fax it here?' ...... 'Yes, see you Wednesday. Bye.'

'It should come through soon, Jack.'

'Thanks again, Sarah.'

'It's a black tie thing, you know,' she said, knowing my hatred of formal wear.

'Don't worry. I'll survive for one evening.'

'Come on downstairs,' she said.

I followed her down to her private office where the fax machine was located. It was already chattering. When it stopped, she handed me three pages of paper.

'I hope you find the name you need,' she said.

I looked down the list, Lord This, Lady That, even a couple of Dukes and the obligatory minor Royal. I continued through and my heart leapt. There it was! Sir Paul Smythe. I passed the sheets back to Sarah, trying not to show my excitement, and said, 'Yes, I will be needing that ticket if you don't mind, Sarah.' She went back to her private quarters and soon reappeared bearing a stiffly monogrammed piece of card which said, 'We request the company of Sandy Richards, PM, at the London Guildhall on etc. etc.'

'The only problem is that the ticket is not transferable,' she said. My heart sank. I hadn't thought of that. But then she continued, 'But if you come as my escort, it will be fine, I promise.'

'I'm already looking forward to it,' I said playfully.

'It'll certainly be more fun than usual,' she replied and, giving my cheek a peck, we parted.

I left No. 10 with a spring in my step and then remembered that I had promised Pamela I would try to be back that morning. I rang Chequers and told Joe I should be back in a couple of hours and to pass on the message to Pamela.

I drove west out of London, not particularly concentrating on the road (I knew the way so well I felt I could drive it blindfold) but thinking of the delights of the warm female body that awaited me. Before I knew it, I was in rural Buckinghamshire. Then I glanced in my mirror and saw a powerful motorbike behind me with a passenger on the pillion behind the rider, both concealed by black visors. Hadn't I seen that bike before in London as I left? Adrenalin rushed in and instinct took over as I accelerated fast. The new engine responded well and all my anti-terrorist driving techniques came back to me as if I had been drilled in them just yesterday.

I pulled the gun out of the glove compartment where I had stashed it, took off the safety catch and laid it on the seat beside me. But still the bike gained on me. I was relying on my familiarity with the road and took the corners too fast but still in control. I looked again in the rear view mirror and saw the passenger take something out of a sports bag he had slung over his shoulder. It looked like a machine pistol, very nasty indeed. The road was empty of traffic. They were now right behind me, preparing to overtake, so I braked hard thinking to throw the rider off balance but he was good and came up next to me. I lifted my own gun and prepared to shoot. But before I could, the passenger raised the machine pistol and raked my borrowed Volvo with bullets.

I ducked and fortunately, as far as I could tell, was not hit but I could feel the car responding more sluggishly. He had obviously hit something important. I raised my head from where I had momentarily hidden it below the level of the window and saw the gunman preparing to shoot again. He had raised his visor, presumably so that he could see me more clearly. I had my own gun in my hand and squeezed the trigger wildly. I could have sworn I saw the bullet leave the gun and smack into the forehead of the gunman, right between the eyes. A direct hit, I thought exultantly. He wobbled on the pillion and then fell off, crashing into the road. The rider of the bike, who was now ahead of me, looked over his shoulder, obviously didn't like what he saw and went racing off into the distance.

I pulled the car to a shaky stop by the side of the road and then got out and went to inspect the gunman. He was dead so I kicked his gun off the road and then rolled his body under some leaves to prevent any ladies of a sensitive disposition who might happen to pass from having hysterics. I knew I had been incredibly lucky and couldn't afford to drop my guard again.

I wasn't far from Chequers now so I rang Joe and told him tersely what had happened. 'Stay right where you are, sir,' he said. 'We'll be along shortly to clear up the mess.' Then I checked myself all over but, apart from a few scratches and a bullet graze on the head, I seemed to be fine. I bandaged the graze, which was bleeding, as best I could, using a sleeve from my shirt. I must look a fright, I thought morosely, and then wondered what Pamela would say.

Joe and some of his soldier mates turned up shortly, as he had said he would, in two cars with a tow truck following closely behind. Joe put me in the car he was driving and the others unceremoniously bundled the body of the gunman into the boot of theirs while the truck prepared to tow the Volvo away. The whole operation took no more than five minutes and I had still not seen any other traffic on the minor road. Then Joe got back in and prepared to take me back to Chequers.

'You do get into some scrapes, don't you, sir?' he said but the question didn't require an answer and I allowed my head to rest against the headrest, doubtless sullying it with blood. The draining of the adrenalin must have put me to sleep because I woke up in the forecourt of Chequers with Pamela fussing over me like my mother had when I came home after getting scratches on my face from playing Cowboys and Indians in the briar patch behind our house.

'What have you been up to?' she asked angrily.

'I nearly got killed but instead I killed my assailant,' I summarised succinctly.

'Well, come inside and we'll get you cleaned up,' she said, choosing to ignore my explanation of what I had been up to and sounding even more like my mother. She took my arm and led me tottering slightly, faint from blood loss, back inside the house. She administered to my wounds efficiently and I asked her if she had been a nurse in the SAS but she just smiled and carried on with her work. After she had cleaned all the blood off me, she said, 'I think you need a few stitches in your head. I'll call the doctor.' He arrived quickly and tut-tutted over me but didn't ask any questions and stitched me up. As he left, he said, 'Take it easy for a few days, OK?' I waved goodbye and then remembered something vital. I called Joe and asked him where the Volvo was.

He said, 'In the knackers' yard, sir.'

'I want you to go down there right away and retrieve my case from the boot. Have you got my gun and the would-be killer's?'

'Yes, sir, I have. And sorry, sir, I forgot you must have a case. Does it contain anything important?'

'Yes, some very valuable papers which, if they got into the wrong hands, could be fatal.'

'I'll see to it right away.'

'Thanks, Joe. I don't need any more deaths on my conscience.' We both hung up and I sat there fretting with Pamela watching me solicitously.

Joe got back to me within three quarters of an hour to say that he had managed to retrieve my case just in time from the predations of the car crusher. Apparently the car wasn't worth repairing. I breathed a huge sigh of relief and thanked him and he said he would be back with it asap. When he returned, I opened the case to find all my precious originals printed out from Sir Maurice's computer nestling safely in the bottom under my clothes still in their box file. I thanked him again as he handed me my gun back and told him that when this was all over, I would make sure his mate to whom the car had belonged, would at the very least get a new one. He said his mate would be pleased to hear that. And then he left.

I was alone with Pamela again, feeling stronger now, and she appraised me carefully.

'I think you need some food,' she said.

'I need something else more than food,' I said, grabbing her by the waist and tumbling her on the bed. We tore each other's clothes off and made mad, passionate love. When we were both sated, we just lay there holding hands.

'That was nice,' I said kissing her and thinking that if anybody had ever doubted that middle-aged people could have fun in bed, here was the proof.

'More than nice,' she replied, snuggling up next to me. Then I fell asleep, drained of everything, and slept till Monday evening. When I woke up, Pamela wasn't there but she had left me a note saying, 'I think I might love you.' This was the sweetest thing anybody had said to me since Jenny's death and I folded the note and put it carefully inside my wallet. Then I got up and looked at myself in the mirror. I looked like a Sikh with a large turban of bandage around my head. I took it off gently and saw a livid scar but no blood so I showered, changed and then, feeling more presentable, went across to Pamela's room and knocked. She opened the door, looking as fresh as a daisy and gave me a big hug saying, 'You look much better than you did and I like the scar. It makes you look like a warrior.'

'Thanks. I feel much better too. I think I must have needed the sleep. I'm hungry now. Shall we eat?'

Pamela rang down to Chef who said 'Give me a few minutes, Miss B.' We went downstairs together arm in arm and outside where I breathed in deeply. 'It's good to feel safe,' I said. We strolled around the house for a while and then wandered back into the small dining room where Chef had, as usual, concocted the most delicious meal for the two of us, in spite of having had so little warning. He looked at the scar on my head but said nothing. The soul of discretion, as always. He appeared to be genuinely pleased that we now seemed to be an 'item'. I ate like a starving wolf until I couldn't eat another thing. Together we had polished off a couple of excellent bottles of wine from the cellar and I was feeling sleepy again.

As we went upstairs, I knew that I needed to clarify my thoughts on what I had to do the next day so, pleading old age, I excused myself from Pamela, went into my room and got out my trusty notebook. I made a few notes and then, feeling the food and wine doing their work, changed out of my clothes and lay down in bed. I was soon asleep again.

Chapter 22 Tuesday to Wednesday pm

I slept dreamlessly and woke up determined to finish this thing as soon as I could. After I had done my morning ablutions, I went down to the breakfast room, ate alone and then walked over to the Guard House. I found Joe there, staring into an empty cup of coffee. He jumped up and said, 'Good to see you looking better, sir. What can I do for you?'

'I presume you searched the body before disposing of it.'

'Yes, sir. But no ID, I'm afraid. And no mobile phone either.'

'Damn. I presume the other guy must have had it with him.'

'I assume so, sir.'

'Have you sent his prints off to be ID'ed?'

'Yes, sir. But nothing yet.'

'He's probably just another hired hit man,' I mused. Joe didn't bother to reply. 'Let me know if you hear anything.'

'Yes, sir.'

'There are a couple of other things you can help me with. First, I need a tuxedo and all the trimmings. I'm going to a big bash in London tomorrow night.'

'We should be able to find something, sir.'

'And second, I need to be unobtrusive when I am in London. Any ideas?'

His forehead puckered in concentration and then he said, 'What about a disguise, sir?'

I kicked myself for not thinking of that and said, 'Good idea. Do you have any wigs and theatre make-up lying around?'

'I don't think so, sir. But I can send somebody into Aylesbury to get some.'

'I would be grateful, Joe. I'd like to make myself look a lot older.' I said, reckoning that Pamela should be able to help me.

'OK, sir. Will do. I think I have your measurements.'

I gave him them anyway and he went off to run my errands. Meanwhile I went downstairs to pay the captain a visit in his cell. He was staring morosely at the bare walls and I spoke to him through the bars.

'Are they treating you OK?'

He looked at me and grunted which I took to mean Yes.

'Anything you'd like to relieve the boredom?'

'A young stud would be nice. Or failing that a chess set.'

'I'll see to it. I still haven't decided what to do with you.'

'You could always let me go.'

'It's true. I could. But I'm not going to. Not yet anyway.'

I left after asking the guard who was watching him to find him a chess set. I knew I had some phone calls to make so I went back to the office. First I rang Sandy who said, 'I'm glad Sarah can help with the investigation. Any news?'

'Somebody took a pot-shot at me yesterday but, as you can hear, I'm fine.'

'Good. That's a relief. Are you any closer to solving the problem?'

'Maybe. It depends how tomorrow evening goes. Sandy, there is one thing you can help me with. I need help to get back to London. Could you send me a car and a couple of outriders to collect me from Chequers tomorrow afternoon?'

'Yes, that should be easy enough.'

'Thanks. And one word of warning: I'll be arriving at No. 10 in disguise. So don't be surprised when you see me.'

'OK, Jack. Go carefully. See you tomorrow.'

Next I rang Sam. 'Anything else happened at your end?' I asked.

'The schematics on the wall of the house are interesting. My experts tell me that, once set up correctly, the computers those guys had there could have hacked into any database in the country.'

'So you were right in your guess about cyber-terrorists?'

'It looks like it but where on earth did those schematics come from?'

'I should be closer to answering that question soon,' I said.

'Exactly the reply I was hoping to get,' said Sam.

'A couple of other things: first, has the minder said anything?'

'No, nothing at all except that he wants a lawyer.'

'I would be *very* interested to know how that odd phone number got into his mobile.'

'You will be the first to know if we can crack him.'

'Thanks. Second, I promised the young computer expert immunity. Could you have the letter drafted but not signed and shown to him? It should encourage his cooperation.'

'I heard about your offer to him. Yes, I'll do that.'

'One other thing: It might be prudent to have a small team of armed plain clothes detectives on duty at the Guildhall tomorrow evening. I will be there as a guest and could do without any aggro. And finally, have a SWAT team standing by in Gloucester at the same time to await my orders.'

'That's two things, Jack. You are becoming quite a burden to the taxpayer, you know.'

'Sorry about that. If you want results, you have to pay for them, I'm afraid.'

'I know, I know. I was only joking. Yes, of course I'll see to those things for you. But be careful, Jack. We could do without any more carnage on the streets of London.'

We said our goodbyes and hung up. I hurried up to Pamela's room and, after knocking, was summoned inside. She was sitting by the window reading as usual.

'How would you like to go out for din-ner?' I asked.

'You mean out as in outside?'

'That's exactly what I mean, yes.'

'Oh, I'd love that! But I thought we were both still in danger.'

'Yes, it's true. But if we were in disguise and had a couple of Joe's best minders with us, I reckon we should be OK.'

'In disguise?' she asked, puzzled.

'I thought you told me you were a master of disguise.'

'Yes, that's true. But I don't have any of my make-up with me.'

'Don't worry about that. I've asked Joe to get hold of some. I thought we could go as an elderly couple although I'd rather you didn't go as the Queen.'

'That's a great idea,' she chuckled.

'You're going to have to give me some classes in how to act old.'

'I thought you did a pretty good imitation of that last night,' she laughed. I laughed with her and we quickly found ourselves on the bed doing what came naturally to both of us now. When we got up, I looked at my watch and was surprised to see it was already 12.00.

'You see how time flies when you're having fun,' she said mischievously. I smacked her on her bare bottom and left, saying I'd be back shortly. I went downstairs and rang Joe who said that the stuff had just arrived. He would bring it over. He came carrying a large box with a couple of grey wigs in it and a bunch of make-up.

I thanked him and carried the box up to Pamela's room. She squealed with delight when she saw the contents.

'Exactly what I need,' she said. 'Shall I do you first?'

'Go ahead. I'm looking forward to seeing what I look like in twenty years time.'

She finished remarkably quickly, put a wig on me and stood back to admire her handiwork. She said, 'Not bad. Do you want to see yourself now, old man?' I nodded and got up to look at myself in the mirror. It was an astonishing transformation! She had covered the scar on my head with make-up and I had acquired many natural-looking wrinkles. I looked completely different. The wig felt a bit hot but it helped to make me look like an 80-year-old gentleman with a bit of money behind him, exactly the impression I had been hoping to create. 'Perfect,' I cried and hugged her. 'Now do yourself.'

I watched carefully as she applied the make-up in the triptych mirror on her dressing table but she did it so confidently and quickly that I couldn't keep up with the brush strokes. It was like watching a master painter at work or, more precisely, a master forger. Very soon she turned to me and said, 'How's that?' 'What about your hair?' I asked. She quickly put it up in a severe-looking bun and I was looking at a different woman entirely. 'It's a pity I don't have a wig too,' she said. 'You don't need one,' I reassured her. Then I said, 'Let's go downstairs and scare the staff.' She giggled and followed me down.

We went to the kitchen and Chef was so amazed at seeing two people he had never met before in his own domain that he nearly dropped the saucepan he was holding. 'Can we have some lunch soon, Chef?' I asked. He looked more carefully at me and then said, 'Is that you, sir?' My normal voice reassured him that it was indeed me and could I introduce a certain Miss B. to him? Pamela dropped a curtsy and said in an old lady's voice, 'Pleased to meet you.' Chef muttered to himself something about never having seen anything like it and then, more normally, 'Lunch will be served in fifteen minutes, sir and madam.' We left the kitchen and, in the time before lunch, went to find Joe. He was bustling about outside and his jaw dropped open when he saw us. 'Don't worry, Joe,' I said. 'It's only us.' He looked relieved and said, 'If it hadn't been, I would have had to shoot you both.'

Pamela smiled and said, 'I'm glad you didn't have to do that, Joe.'

Then I said, 'I'd really like to take Miss B. to a nice restaurant outside tonight. Could you provide transport and a couple of minders please?'

He looked dubious but when I said 'You didn't recognise us, did you, Joe?' he agreed to book somewhere nice for us. 'And can you get us some more clothes as befitting an elderly couple?' I asked, looking at my now battered suit and Pamela's frock which showed off all her curves.

'Yes, sir,' he said.

We went back inside to find lunch almost ready and we ate in silence, appreciating every mouthful. We just drank water. When we had finished, Pamela said, 'We'll have to do some work on your voice and your gait.' I agreed and we went back upstairs to practise. She made my voice more quavery and taught me to stoop when I walked saying, 'We'll have to get you a stick.' We found one in a coat stand downstairs left by some forgotten gentleman, and I practised walking and talking in my new voice until Pamela pronounced herself satisfied. Then I said that I had to go back to London on Wednesday where I would be putting into practice everything she had taught me. 'I thought there must be some sort of ulterior motive to all this,' she said rather bitterly. Then I told her that I hoped it would be the final act of the drama I had got myself involved in and she cheered up. 'Come to bed,' she said and so I did.

Evening came and she renewed the make-up. Then Joe turned up with the clothes and we changed quickly. I wore a smart but old-fashioned suit, a linen shirt with cufflinks monogrammed with the crest of some forgotten regiment and a sober tie while Pamela put on a frumpish dress which put twenty years on her automatically. We were ready. I collected my stick, stuck my pistol into my belt at the back and went down to the car. It was a black, highly-polished, luxury Daimler which rode very low. Armour-plated, I thought. It must be one of Sandy's official cars he kept at Chequers for visiting dignitaries. It came complete with a chauffeur in a peaked cap, one of Joe's guys I remembered, and Joe himself dressed up to the nines in a smart city suit which hid the bulge under his left arm. 'I'm coming with you,' he said grimly.

In the car on the way Joe turned to us from the front seat where he was sitting and said, 'Don't worry about paying the bill, sir. It's on the country.' I thanked him, thinking that I was forcing up the country's debt rather quickly. We headed through rural Buckinghamshire for about half an hour and pulled into the car park of a lovely old pub by a river. The chauffeur opened the door for us and Joe preceded us into the pub. He had booked a private room for the three of us but kept to himself in a corner while we ate and chatted in our new voices. The meal was excellent, as was the service, and we washed it down with a bottle of first class wine recommended by the wine waiter. Only one bottle, Pamela had warned me. Elderly people don't drink much. 'It's one reason they have lived so long,' I had joked. At one point during the meal Pamela put her hand on mine and whispered, 'This is my most unusual first date ever.' 'Mine too,' I whispered back. We waited while Joe paid the bill and left the pub, walking back arm in arm to the car which was attracting admiring glances from other drivers. On the way back I asked Joe if he had had to do that type of escort duty often. 'Occasionally, sir,' was all he said.

The journey back to Chequers was uneventful and, when we got there, Pamela jumped out and impulsively gave Joe a hug. Embarrassed, he broke free and said, 'What was that for, Miss B.?' 'For giving us such a nice evening, Joe.' 'Yes, thanks, Joe,' I echoed. 'That's all right, sir, ma'am,' he muttered and sloped off into the night.

We went on up to our respective rooms but, as I was about to enter mine, Pamela turned to me and said shyly, 'Would you like to share mine? I've got plenty of room.' I looked at her, realising what she was saying. We were to be a proper married couple now, while at Chequers anyway. My hesitation lasted only a second, however, before I said, 'Yes, I would like that very much.'

So I moved in with her and the next day passed in a haze of sex and preparations for the evening's confrontation. Joe delivered my tuxedo and I must say that I did look rather good in it, a view Pamela agreed with. But I knew I shouldn't get too used to all this high living. I would come down to earth with a bump once all this was over. I also read through all the documents again on Smythe, looking for a more direct connection with banking but finding nothing new. I wondered whether the demand to scrap the limitations on bankers' bonuses was just a smokescreen or whether there really was a conspiracy here with Sir Paul in alliance with other financial people unknown. If he was the head of the Hydra though, that was good enough for me. And Pamela continued to work on my voice and gait until I actually felt like an elderly gentleman. I was as prepared as I could be for the evening ahead.

Chapter 23
Wednesday pm

My potential killer's ID had come through in the morning and I had been right. Another contract marksman. They all seemed to be coming out of the wood-work now. But I wasn't going to be distracted by thoughts of my potentially early demise and I focussed on the task in hand. I knew once I was inside the Guildhall, I would have to play it by ear but I reckoned I could take out anybody, provided that they had not had black arts training which there was no indication of in Smythe's file.

Wednesday afternoon came round much too quickly and Pamela did my make-up again and fitted the wig after I had changed into the tux. I got the stick and looked in the mirror. I looked every inch the picture of an elderly gentleman, possibly a retired officer in the Army. I was completely unrecognisable which was the main thing. Then the car sent by Sandy arrived, a comfortable Jaguar, and after saying my goodbyes to Pamela and Joe, I left Chequers, my gun nestling in the small of my back.

I was whisked back to Downing Street accompanied by the two police outriders I had requested and deposited outside the front door for a change. It was 6 pm. I went in to be confronted by an aide who obviously didn't recognise me. He asked for my ID and I showed him my MI5 Downing Street pass. He looked at the photo on it, then looked suspiciously back at me and I said, 'It's a very old picture, I'm afraid.' That seemed to satisfy him and I was shown up to Sarah's private quarters where I was told she was getting ready. Sandy wasn't there and I kicked my heels for a while until she appeared, looking radiant. When she saw me, she did a double take and said uncertainly, 'Jack?' 'Yes, it is me. Sorry about the subterfuge,' I said in my normal voice. She came up to me and gave me a hug saying, 'That's OK. I love subterfuge,' and I could smell her perfume. We chatted for a bit and I asked where Sandy was. 'He's around somewhere,' she said, waving her hand vaguely, 'dealing with affairs of state.'

'I hope you've squared my invitation?'

'Of course. I said you were a very old friend of my family who's taking Sandy's place.'

'Perfect. The 'very old' is appropriate, don't you think?'

She grinned and then said she had to pop upstairs to kiss the children good night. When she came back, she grabbed a shawl and we went down to yet another official car which was waiting for us. We got in and were driven to the Guildhall.

I managed to get in by Sarah's side without a problem and looked around. The place was glittering with polished silver and candlelight and I thought rather sourly that the big charities did themselves proud these days. It was also thronged with Establishment figures, some of whom I knew from my time spent in Downing Street and others whom I recognised from newspaper photographs but nobody paid me the slightest attention. Exactly how I wanted it. I had memorised Smythe's photo from his file and I looked around to see if I could spot him but in the crowd it simply wasn't possible. Then we were called to dinner and Sarah and I were led up to the High Table which was literally that, being raised on a dais a little above the rest of the crowd. I sat on Sarah's left and was introduced by her as Jack West to the people on either side of us, as I had asked her to do. One was a Duke and the other the Chairman of the charity, a bluff old guy, Lord Somebody-Something.

I examined the crowd sitting at many round tables below us and then, with a frisson of excitement, I spotted him. He was sitting at the back with a table all to himself except for a burly chap who I reckoned was a minder in spite of his tuxedo. I had seen no sign of Sam's armed detectives but presumed there were at least a couple around somewhere. I had already pinpointed the toilets as the likeliest place to make contact. The dinner progressed smoothly and I made small-talk in my old man's voice with my neighbours. I kept my gaze, however, on the table at the back. The meal itself was eminently forgettable but the wine was good although I drank sparingly.

Then, just as we were finishing pudding, I noticed Smythe say something to his table companion and get up. I excused myself, got my stick and made my old man's way in pursuit. He was heading for the toilets as I had hoped. I got there just behind him and he opened the door for me. I thanked him and we both went up to the urinals. I looked around but the place seemed empty. Perfect! I knew that a man peeing was at his most vulnerable and, standing next to him, asked him mildly, 'Do you recognise me, Sir Paul?' He looked up at me at the mention of his name and said, 'No, never seen you before in my life.'

'I think we need to get to know each other better,' I said. I hadn't even unzipped my flies and I moved behind him and applied pressure to his carotid artery to stop the blood flow to his brain. He lashed out hard but missed and I held on grimly with one arm round his neck until he collapsed. I knew he would be out for a while and I bundled him into the furthest stall. Then I rang Sam and asked him to send his men into the toilets. The whole episode had taken less than two minutes but I knew I had to hurry in case the minder came in, wondering where his master was.

The detectives arrived within about another minute and I pointed at the stall and said, 'We've got to get him out of here fast and discreetly.' They looked at the heavy-set man lying on the stall floor and one of them said, 'We can do the first but I'm not so sure if we can do it discreetly.' Then I had a brainwave. I took off my wig and put it on the unconscious man's head, changing his appearance radically. I said, 'That should make it easier.' The two detectives hauled him up and staggered through the door with him between them. I went in front and saw the minder looking suspiciously at the four of us. Fortunately, he didn't recognise his master immediately and then a few people came over asking if they could help, masking him from view. I said, 'No, don't worry. We'll take him to hospital. Just a mild stroke, I think.' We got outside without incident and I turned to see the minder heading rapidly for the toilets. I knew we had only a couple more minutes, if that, before he called for reinforcements who I guessed would be nearby and probably watching. I said urgently, 'Where's your car?' 'Round the corner,' said one of Sam's men. 'Come on then. Let's hurry,' I said. With me walking fast in front, I rounded the corner and saw a white Ford Mondeo. 'Give me the keys,' I said. One of the men fished them out of his pocket and I opened the car and then the boot. 'Put him in there,' I said. Fortunately there was nobody around to see us and I thought the Fates must still be smiling on me. They managed to cram him in and then the four of us were speeding away from the Guildhall with nobody apparently following.

'Where to, Guv?' asked the driver. I had thought about this already and had decided that the safest place would be MI5's headquarters and I asked him to drive there. Then I phoned Sir Maurice and managed to get him at home. I said, 'I've got the prime suspect and am taking him to your office. Hope that's OK with you.' 'Good man. I'll get everything set up.' When we arrived, I directed the driver down to the basement garage, using my old MI5 pass to open the gates. Inside I found a reception committee waiting for me, consisting of several of my old colleagues. They welcomed me back warmly once they had recognised me under my make-up and I thanked the driver and his mate saying, 'We can take it from here.' My old colleagues then hauled Smythe out of the boot and I waved goodbye to the two detectives. He was conscious by now but still groggy and didn't put up any resistance as we took him up in the lift straight to the interview rooms on the third floor. There they tied him to a chair and handcuffed him to make absolutely sure he didn't cause any trouble. I sent them all out, knowing that they would be watching and listening to what transpired from the other side of the two-way mirror. Then I sat down at the bare table.

He glared at me and said in a bass rumble, 'Where the hell am I?'

'Never mind that. You're safe,' I paused, 'for the moment.'

'I've got friends in very high places. You're going to pay dearly for this.'

'I'm afraid you haven't got any friends here.'

'Who the hell *are* you?'

'Ever heard of a guy called Jack Sanderson?'

He gasped and then said, 'Don't be ridiculous. You're not him.'

'Wait here a moment.' I left and went into a nearby washroom where I got rid of the make-up. Then I went back into the interview room and said, 'Now do you recognise me?'

He blanched and then said, 'What do you want?'

'I'm afraid I'm asking the questions now. Can you confirm for me your name and address?' I said formally, knowing that everything would be going down on tape next door. He reeled them off as if he was a prisoner-of-war giving his name, rank and serial number.

'Thank you. Now, my first question is, Why are you so keen to have me killed?'

No response. Just another glare. I waited, then asked, 'What about Miss Pamela Burrows?'

Again no response. I waited. Eventually he said, 'Can I have a drink of water?'

'Later. You should know that we've got you bang to rights as the coppers used to say in the old movies.'

'You've got nothing on me. Nothing.'

'Oh, I beg to differ. Until quite recently it's true that all the evidence was circumstantial but now we've got hard proof. I'm sure you're aware of the penalties that exist in this country for High Treason. Did you really think you were going to get away with blackmailing the PM and the country into cushioning your and your pals' pockets?'

'I've still got the evidence he wants,' he said almost sulkily.

'But I'm afraid you're not going to have it for long.'

And I took out my mobile phone and rang Sam. I said, 'Sam, that SWAT team you were going to let me have in Gloucester. Are they in place? Good. I'd like you to send them straight away to this address,' and I reeled off Smythe's address, 'and to search it thoroughly. I have a traitor here with me who's going to confess to everything so don't bother about a search warrant. But tell them to be careful. I think there's likely to be armed resistance. On the other hand, there aren't likely to be any civilians there. I want you also to tell them that, if they find any tapes, I need them to be brought back to London and delivered into your hands without being listened to. Got all that? Fine. Thanks, Sam. I'll be in touch later.'

'You can't do that,' he said angrily.

'Oh, I think you'll find I've already done it, *Sir* Paul,' I said, stressing the 'Sir' contemptuously.

'I'm not confessing to anything.'

'You've already admitted to having evidence the PM wants,' I said. 'It shouldn't be difficult now to admit to everything else.' I saw a look of horror cross his face as he realised what he had already admitted to. 'Let's face it, Smythe,' I continued, deliberately leaving out his title, 'We're reaching the end game now for you in this country. You've given us plenty of rope to hang you with.'

He picked up on the three words I hoped he would. 'What do you mean 'in this country'?'

'Well, I was thinking maybe we could do a deal.'

'What kind of deal?' he asked almost eagerly.

'If you confess everything to my colleagues next door, we might just let you go abroad and live off your assets there. We'd have to confiscate all your British ones obviously. And you'd have to promise never to set foot inside Britain again.'

I saw him doing the calculations in his head. Finally, after a lot of consideration, he nodded and said, 'OK. We've got a deal. But I want a promise of immunity while I'm still here.'

I breathed a sigh of relief. He knew which side his bread was buttered on, did Sir Paul. 'You'll get it,' I said, thinking that I was throwing immunities around like confetti. I took out my mobile, rang Sam again and said, 'I've got what I wanted. A clear confession of conspiracy to destabilise the country. But I'm afraid I'll need another certificate of immunity. Can you draft one leaving the name blank and send it straight round to No. 10? I'll be there soon myself.' He agreed to do it, believing I must know what I was doing. I wasn't exactly sure myself if I did or not. I had been bluffing when I said I'd had hard proof but, then, I thought that I was a better poker player than most guys and, anyway, I should be on the brink of getting the proof I needed.

I turned back to Smythe, as I thought of him now, and said, 'I'll be back in the morning with the immunity order. Then I'll be sitting in on your debriefing.' I didn't want to use the word 'interrogation' as I thought he might get second thoughts if I did.

'Fine,' he said morosely.

I left the room and went next door where I asked whether all his answers to my questions could be transferred to another tape and mixed up so that the context wouldn't be clear. I passed across a mini tape recorder I had had in my pocket all evening saying, 'You'll find another sentence on this if you need it,' remembering our first encounter in the toilet of the Guildhall. 'I'll pick it up tomorrow morning.' The tech guy in support said I could have it quicker than that if I wanted but I said that it wasn't necessary. I knew it could be better used in the morning. Then I said, 'Chuck him in a cell overnight to stew. But keep watch over him and don't let him have anything with which he might be able to top himself. I'm off now,' and I left the building.

I got a taxi outside and went straight over to Downing Street. There I was met by the same aide I had met much earlier that evening. He said ironically, 'You look younger, sir.' 'It's all down to clean living,' I replied and he chuckled. He took me up to Sarah's private quarters and I met her there. She was dressed for bed and I apologised for the late hour.

'What happened to you? Why did you abandon me? Was that you I saw leaving with an unconscious man?' The questions all came tumbling out and I said, 'To answer your third question first, yes, I'm afraid that was me you saw and in answer to the other two, I'm sorry but it was state business.' She was about to ask more questions but I put my finger on her lips to hush her and said, 'I need to speak to Sandy urgently.'

'So you're abandoning me again, are you?' she said playfully. And then more seriously. 'As far as I know, he's in his study working. Tell him I'm going to bed.' I said I would and went down to Sandy's study.

I barged right in but he was alone reading something. 'I need your full attention, Sandy,' I said.

'You've got it, Jack,' putting what he was reading down.

'I should have my final proof that Sir Paul Smythe is the head of the conspiracy tomorrow morning. Meanwhile he's tucked up somewhere safe.'

'That's very good news, Jack. Well done!' he said, beaming from ear to ear. 'What happened to the tapes?'

'They should be winging their way towards me now,' I said, crossing my fingers that I had been right and they were in Smythe's house and remembering at the same time that I had to call Sam again.

'Good. Bring them straight to me please, Jack.'

'Of course. Can I stay here tonight again? I need to be in the centre of things.'

'No problem at all. Anything else?'

'Well, yes. I had to offer him immunity here to get his cooperation but he has agreed to leave the country as soon as his interrogation is over. I presumed you wouldn't want a messy trial. The papers should be here shortly if you could sign them. I'll take them back to him tomorrow morning.'

'You are absolutely right, Jack, about me not wanting a messy trial. The thought of the information on the tapes getting out is enough to make me shudder. So, yes, of course I'll sign the papers if you can guarantee that I get back every last copy of them.'

'It's difficult to give guarantees, Sandy, but I'm doing my best.'

'I know you are.'

Just then there was a knock on the door and an aide came in carrying an envelope. 'This just came in from Scotland Yard, Prime Minister,' he said.

'Thanks, Peter. I've been waiting for it.' He opened the envelope, read the papers quickly, signed his name three times and passed them back to me saying, 'I wonder how much these are worth on the black market.'

I grinned and said, 'A lot of money at a guess,' and took them from him. Then I said, 'I've got a few more loose ends to tie up tonight. So I'll leave you in peace. Oh, and Sarah's gone to bed.' I left Sandy, clutching the papers, and went up to my old room. It was ready for visitors as always and I lay on the bed and called Sam, knowing that, because of all the excitement, he would still be in his office. 'What news from the team, Sam?' I asked.

'Straight to business, eh, Jack. No sympathy for keeping an old man out of his warm bed?'

'I'm sorry for keeping you up, Sam,' I sighed. 'Now please answer my question.'

'Quite a lot, actually. The team had some trouble accessing the house. There was a fire fight and two of our guys were wounded, not fatally, I hasten to add. They managed to kill the shooters and then, when they got to the house, they found it heavily alarmed. It's quite isolated, you know.'

'I presume they managed to get in in the end?'

'Yes, but it took a while. They found a computer in the study which has been taken away for analysis, a lot of valuable stuff, paintings and the like, and a big box of tapes in a safe in the master bedroom.'

'Have you got them?'

Yes, they just arrived along with a bunch of fake passports and other stuff useful to criminals. Who *was* this guy, Jack?'

'Somebody MI5 has been interested in for quite a while. Can you get the tapes to me at No. 10 tonight, please?'

'They *are* important, aren't they?'

'They, hopefully, are the reason for this entire investigation.'

'I'll drive them to you myself. I should be there in about 15 minutes. There's not much traffic around at the moment.'

'Thanks, Sam. I'll meet you at the entrance to Downing Street.' I went downstairs and left by the front door, telling the doorman I'd be back soon with something for the PM. Then I sauntered down the empty street, was let through the gates and loitered outside. In less than fifteen minutes I saw Sam's police Rover pull up. He got out, opened the boot and gave me a heavy box.

'Can I go to bed now, please, sir?' he enquired ironically.

'Yes, you run along and I'll be in touch soon. Thanks for everything, Sam.'

He grunted and drove off at high speed in the direction of his Wimbledon home. I staggered with the heavy box back through the gates, up the street and back into No. 10. 'You're fitter than me,' I said, breathing heavily, to the ex-Marine who was the doorman. 'Can you carry this up to the PM's study please?' He didn't respond but looked at me with the contempt the young have for the middle-aged and the elderly.

Then he lifted the box under one brawny arm and bounded up the stairs two at a time. I followed more slowly puffing a bit. I knocked on the door, thanked the doorman who saluted me (rather sloppily, I thought) and went in carrying the box.

'Is that it?' Sandy asked.

'Yes, I hope so,' I said. 'Some policemen went to a lot of trouble to get it.'

He opened the box, which was only cardboard, and took out a Jiffy bag with 'Daily Mail' written on it. He opened the bag and tipped a mini cassette tape onto the desk. He took out more bags. They had the names of all the major British media outlets on them with their addresses and quite a few important foreign ones as well. He dumped the whole lot on the desk and, right at the bottom, one fell out labelled 'master copy'. He gave a yell of triumph and fitted it into a tape recorder.

I heard his voice say, 'Gentlemen and lady (presumably referring to Pamela) we all know why we are here. To discuss a matter of grave national importance. Namely, what might happen if the Queen gets seriously ill or, God forbid, dies.' He switched it off, clapped me on the back and said, 'That's it, Jack. Many, many thanks.'

'You owe me quite a bit in expenses, you know,' I said.

'Worth every penny,' he said.

Aren't you going to play the rest?' I asked, curious to know why he had switched it off after only listening to a few sentences.

'That's OK, Jack. It's the right tape. I know it is. I'm just going to dispose of the lot of them,' waving his hand at the debris strewn on his desk.

'OK. They're your tapes,' I said.

'You go on to bed,' he said, ushering me out. So I went upstairs to my bedroom, looked at my watch -12.45 – and crashed out without even taking my clothes off. I got up in the middle of the night to pee and crawl out of my tuxedo and then went back to sleep till I was woken at 8 am by a maid who offered me breakfast on a tray and the morning Times.

Chapter 24 Thursday

Having showered, changed and had breakfast, I headed out of No. 10 via the tunnel and caught a taxi in Whitehall. I asked the driver to take me straight to MI5 headquarters on the South Bank. En route, I rang Chequers and asked to speak to Pamela. She berated me for not ringing her the night before, saying she had stayed up half the night worrying about me. I apologised (I seemed to be doing an awful lot of that lately) saying I really had been extremely busy. I could hear tears in her voice and I hoped they were tears of relief as she said, 'Thank God you're OK. How did it go?'

'Swimmingly thanks. Better than I expected. It should all be over soon. All being well, I may be able to come back this afternoon.'

'That would be lovely.'

We were approaching MI5 and I said, 'I have to ring off now. Sorry again.'

'That's OK, Jack. But don't you dare ever worry me like that again!' Just like my mother or even an angry wife?

'I'll try not to, I promise. Bye,' and I blew her a kiss over the phone. I heard one coming down the line to me and then we both hung up. I knew I had to concentrate now so I tried to put all thoughts of Pamela out of my head but they always seemed to be lurking somewhere in my subconscious.

I went in after showing my ID and on up to the third floor where I met the tech support guy. 'Have you got the tape?' I asked without preamble. 'Yes, sir,' and he took a micro cassette out of his pocket. 'Good. I'd like to listen to it.' So he popped it into a tiny player and pressed Play. Smythe's voice came through as clear as a bass bell and his sentences were suitably confused so that nobody would be able to recognise the whole context of what he was saying. 'Good job,' I said. 'Can I borrow the player and an empty office with a secure phone?'

'By all means,' and he led me down the hall to an office marked Director of Overseas Operations which was empty. 'You shouldn't be disturbed in here,' he said. Then he added, 'Sir Maurice is in and would like to see you at your earliest convenience.'

'OK. I'll see him when I've finished in here. How's the prisoner?'

'Not saying much, I hear. Missing his mum probably.'

'OK. I'll deal with him after I've seen Sir M. Tell the team to be on stand-by.'

'Yes, sir.' And he left me alone.

What I was about to do was, for me, the most crucial phase of the whole operation. I needed proof that Smythe had personally ordered the killing of myself and Pamela. I wanted to be able to accuse him of attempted murder so badly I could taste it. It really made me angry that somebody, with a single phone call, could be able to try so determinedly to kill us both. If he could be charged with other murders along the way, so much the better. But it was the personal angle that rankled so much. I had more or less forgotten about the tapes and the treachery. And to get him to confess, I needed the doctored tape and the little machine.

First, I rang Joe who seemed pleased to hear from me. I asked him to bring the captain up from his cell and to tell him to be prepared to take a phone call from me. I would stay on the line. Joe did as I asked and I was soon talking to the captain.

'Is your chess improving?' I asked.

He laughed and said, 'I hope so. I've certainly had enough time to practise.'

'I want you to do something for me,' I said. 'I'd like you to listen to another tape and tell me truthfully if this is the man who gave you your orders.'

'OK.'

I played him the tape and said, when it had finished, 'Is that him?'

'I ...I think so,' he said uncertainly, 'but I couldn't be 100% sure.'

'That's OK. Don't worry about it,' I said. I was disappointed but not completely disheartened. I knew I had two more bites at the cherry. I thanked Joe and hung up.

Then I looked in my notebook for the number in Scotland where the two mercenaries were being held. I knew that even the major players in the criminal underworld liked to get their own hands dirty occasionally and was banking on the fact that it was Smythe himself who had given the orders to have us killed and not some underling. I got through easily to the girl I had spoken to before with the nice Scottish accent and asked to be connected to the Colonel who was responsible for my two mercenaries. He came to the phone and I asked how they had been behaving. He chuckled and said, 'Not much chance of them misbehaving in here.'

'I'd like you to bring them to the phone one at a time. I have something for them to listen to.'

'OK. Hang on.'

It was a few minutes later that I heard Barnard's South African accent. 'When are you getting us out of here?' he demanded.

'All in good time,' I said. 'Remember you're in there for your own protection. I'm sure you don't want MI6 crawling all over you.'

That shut him up and I went through exactly the same rigmarole as I had done with the captain. This time I hit pay dirt! I didn't even have to play the whole recording when he broke in and said decisively, 'That's him. I'd swear to it.'

'Do you mean that?' I asked.

'Yes,' he said.

'OK. I'm going to ask the Colonel to take a formal statement from you to that effect. Is that all right with you?'

'Yes, I suppose so.'

When the Colonel came back on the line, I told him I was ready for Eiger. I didn't have to wait long for him and went through the whole thing for the third time that morning. He too was decisive in his recognition of the voice. I had got what I wanted and told the Colonel to take statements, signed and sealed, from both of them and to forward them to me asap at MI5 in London. Then I said to him, 'I have no further use for them. If you can deport them discreetly back to South Africa, I'd be very grateful.' He said that that should be possible and we both hung up. Another problem solved and duty discharged.

Now I could concentrate on the meeting with the devious Sir Maurice. I went up to his office on the top floor and was let in straight away.

'Are you going to tell me now what's been going on?' he demanded.

'Most of it,' I said and proceeded to give him a bowdlerised account of everything that had happened since the Sunday before last. He kept his eyes on me the whole time and, when I had finished, said, 'You always were my best student, Jack. We've been after this bugger for ages but it took you to bring him down. I've a mind to let you have your old job back.'

'Thanks, Sir M. But I'd better take a rain check on that. I've got other plans in the meantime.'

'Would they include the delectable Miss Burrows?' he asked perspicaciously.

'Maybe,' I said blushing.

'Well, the very best of luck to you, Jack. Now I believe you have a prisoner to interrogate.'

'Yes, I do,' I said, getting up from my chair. 'One last thing though. You remember how my file disappeared?' He nodded and I continued, 'Have you checked to see what other files might have gone missing?'

He smacked his forehead in self-disgust and said, 'I really should have thought of that. I'll get on to it right away.'

'No reason to castigate yourself,' I said. 'Remember you thought your system was fool-proof.'

'I know,' he said ruefully. 'I'll get any details to you as soon as I get them myself.'

'Thanks. I think it might be useful.' And I left.

Now it was Smythe's turn. I went down to the third floor where the rest of the team were waiting and looked through the two-way mirror at him. He was hand-cuffed again and looking the worse for wear, his tuxedo crumpled, his bowtie missing, as were his shoelaces, and he was unshaven. 'Everything set up?' I asked pointing to the banks of recording equipment around us. The tech guy nodded and I said, 'Take the cuffs off him please.' I followed a member of the team into the room who removed his handcuffs, waited till he had left and sat down opposite Smythe.

'Did they give you that drink of water you wanted?' I asked.

He nodded and said, 'Have you got that immunity letter?'

I said yes and took it out of the bag I had with me. He perused it greedily and finally said, 'Good.'

'OK? Now let's get started. Soon, remember, you'll be off to soak up the sun with a bunch of dancing girls if I'm not mistaken.' I saw his eyes gleam and knew I had hit the target. 'First I'd like to clear up the small matter of why you wanted so badly to see myself and Miss Burrows dead. I have the proof that you ordered the killings personally.'

'You can't have,' he breathed.

'Yes, I can. You remember the two mercenaries you sent to kill Miss Burrows? They have positively ID'ed your voice giving the orders. Silly of you really not to have left the job to an underling. But the best-laid plans of mice and men, eh?' He looked defeated now and I pressed home my question. 'So why did you want us dead?'

'Because I knew that Miss Burrows had been in the SAS and you had had plenty of MI5 training and, after the cathedral, I perceived you both as a major threat to my plans.'

'How did you know Miss Burrows had been in the SAS?'

'I had seen her file just like I had seen yours.'

I knew I had been right to ask Sir M. to have another look at the filing system.

'OK. That all makes sense. Now, before I leave you to the tender mercies of the guys behind the mirror,' I said, pointing behind him, 'there is one more thing you can do for me. Cancel the contract on us.' And I passed him my mobile phone. He looked at it as if he had never seen one before but then, after a long pause, dialled a number.

I heard him say, 'The contract's off.' He listened for a bit and then said, 'Don't worry about me. I'm OK. But I no longer want Miss Burrows or Jack Sanderson killed. Is that clear?' I heard a squawky voice say, 'Yes,' and then he broke the connection.

'Who was that?' I asked innocently.

'My top aide, Toby. He's at the air-port waiting to leave the country,' he said bitterly.

I knew the team would have picked this up and already be alerting the airports. Rats leaving a sinking ship, I thought.

'How did you get on to me in the first place?' he asked.

'Your ring,' I said shortly, wondering if he would be able to work out his mistake. Then I said, 'I think that just about concludes my business with you.' And I stood up and left the room.

I passed Sir Maurice himself with a large sheaf of papers just about to go in and knew that Smythe would be wrung dry before he could leave the country. He winked at me and said in an undertone, 'Thanks for softening him up, Jack.' I waved goodbye, left the third floor and went down to the basement. There I asked the dispatcher if I could borrow a car for a day or so. I would get somebody to drive it back but I needed it to retrieve my own car. He agreed readily, knowing I was in favour with Sir M. again, and I signed the papers and was soon on my way, this time back to Downing Street.

When I got there, I was just in time to catch Sandy who was off back to his constituency for the evening. He had to deliver a speech, he said. I asked if he could give me a few minutes before he left. He took me up to his private office and we sat down.

'How did it go with Sir Paul?' he asked.

'Fine,' I said. 'Everything's been sorted. Sir Maurice is interrogating him now.'

'Good. Is there anything else I can do?'

'Yes. You can give me a largish cheque for my expenses. It's mainly for a new car for somebody. I pranged his old one in the line of duty.'

'Of course. How much do you want?'

I mentioned a sum and he immediately wrote me a private cheque for the amount.

'Thanks,' I said. Then I asked, 'Are you happy with the outcome of this whole thing?'

'Why on earth wouldn't I be? You've done a superlative job for me.'

'I was thinking of the fact that a murderer and master criminal is going to get away scot free.'

'It can't be helped, Jack.'

I thought of the pragmatism of politicians but just said, 'Sir Maurice has offered me my old job back.'

'That's great.'

'Yes, I suppose so,' I said uncertainly. 'Actually I turned him down. There is still one thing that puzzles me about all this but as I don't think it's relevant to National Security, I won't detain you.'

'OK. My door is always open to you. You know that, don't you, Jack?'

'Yes,' I said and we parted.

This time I drove to my bank in Westminster and deposited the cheque. There was one more errand I had to run in London and I drove to New Scotland Yard. There I was shown up to Sam's office. He was in as I knew he would be and I said, 'It's all over, Sam, bar the shouting.'

'That's very good. So no more carnage on the streets?'

'No. I'm here to retrieve the documents I left with you,' I said.

'Sure. Wait here a few minutes.'

I sat in his office and mulled over the rest of the loose ends. When he returned, he had with him all my papers. I stuffed them into my shoulder bag and said, 'Many thanks for all your help, Sam.'

'That's OK, matey. Any time. All the excitement actually made me feel younger. Oh, by the way, a dickey bird told me that the Prime Suspect in all this is being interrogated at MI5. We've got some stuff from the house and his computer which might help. Should I send it all over there?'

'It's your decision, Sam, but I think it would be a good idea,' I said, thinking of the usual rivalry between the two organisations. 'I reckon there will be a few major criminal trials coming up soon.'

'That's what I suspected,' he said.

We shook hands and I left. I went back to the car and looked at my watch. I had missed lunch again! I put the documents in the boot and phoned Pamela, saying that I would be later than I had expected and to have lunch without waiting for me. There were no complaints this time. She just said to hurry back. I drove back to Chequers at a leisurely pace, thinking of the things I still had to do. I stopped off once at a greasy spoon to have a bite to eat and it was about 5 pm when I finally reached the gates of the estate. Instead of driving directly to the main house, I went instead to the guard house looking for Joe. I found him there and after his usual hail-fellow-well-met greeting, I said, 'I've been thinking, Joe, of what to do with our troublesome captain. We can't keep him locked up here for ever.'

'Yes, sir?' He looked at me expectantly.

'I think he was severely pressured into his crime and that it was something he would never normally think of doing. So I reckon the best thing would be to give him an honourable discharge from the Army and give him a leg up to find a decent job in Civvy Street.'

'That's very kind of you, sir, considering that he tried to kill you.'

'I know he did but he didn't succeed, did he?'

'I'll set the wheels in motion tomorrow morning, sir.'

'Thanks, Joe. There are a couple of other things too. I want you to go out with your mate, the one whose car got shot up, and get him a new one. He can go up to fifty grand.'

That really is kind of you, sir. He will be delighted, I'm sure.'

'Bill it to me and tell him not to worry. It's not my money.'

'Will do, sir.'

'One last thing: Miss B. and I will be leaving tomorrow to return to London. I'd like to take my own car back with me so could you arrange for somebody to take the car I came in back to MI5 headquarters for me?'

'I'm sure that can easily be arranged, sir. Does this mean that you're both in the clear now?'

'Sorry. I forgot you haven't been in the loop. Yes, that's exactly what it means. Everything's been sorted.'

'I'm very glad, sir.'

'So am I, Joe, so am I.' And I left him to return to the main house and Pamela.

Pamela was going to be my biggest loose end, I knew. I went in, dreading the next few minutes. I went up to her room and nearly knocked as usual but then remembered that it was my room now as well as hers. I entered and she was there reading. She jumped up as I came in and flung herself into my arms. A strange mixture of emotions flooded through me: protectiveness, distrust and even love. I held her away from me and looked at her. 'You're looking well, Pamela,' I said. And indeed she had a youthful, rosy flush to her cheeks. She stood back and appraised me carefully. Then she said, 'Is that all you've got to say to me?'

'We've got to talk, Pamela,' I said.

She sat down on the bed and said carefully, 'OK. So talk.'

'First, I need to tell you something I found out what seems like ages ago from Sir Maurice.' I continued, 'He hypnotised you into forgetting the surgeon and all the trauma that went with the surgery. I'm sorry I didn't tell you earlier. There just never seemed to be a right time.'

Her eyes blazed and she got up and started to pace. 'That old bastard,' she said angrily.

'I know he can be a bastard,' I said soothingly. 'And you have every right to be angry with him. But I hope you won't do anything rash like bringing a lawsuit against him. You could, you know. It's highly illegal to hypnotise anyone against their will. But I hope you won't. He did it because he wasn't sure whether if you knew all the gory details, you'd be willing to go along with the plan.'

She said, still angrily, 'That bastard,' but with less feeling this time.

'The good news now,' I said. 'We're both off the hook. Nobody is going to try to kill us any more.'

'Oh, fantastic! Why didn't you tell me earlier?'

'I wanted to tell you in person.' That seemed to satisfy her.

Then she said suspiciously, 'Is that all?'

'No, not quite. Another bit of good news. I think your file's disappeared form Central Registry in MI5. This means that your entire past has been erased. So you can start again. At least, I hope it's good news.'

'But Sir Maurice still knows all about me,' she said perspicaciously.

'Yes, of course he does. But he's the only one apart from the PM. And I don't think he will reveal any details of your army training or what you supposedly did for the country.'

'Because of the fact that I might prosecute him. OK. I suppose that's good news in a way. But why do I get the impression you've kept the worst till last?'

I took a deep breath and said, 'Yes, I suppose I have. I think you've had an affair with Sandy who also happens to be my oldest friend.'

Her face lost all its colour. It looked as if she had been slapped hard and I thought she might faint. I knew I had been in self-denial ever since I had heard the hesitation in their voices when I asked them about their first meeting. I hadn't been able to believe that it would be possible for Sandy to have betrayed Sarah so callously. I had always thought they had the happiest marriage possible but then, who knows anything about other people? It was only in Sandy's office that morning that I had put two and two together. It had been the only possible explanation for Sandy not wanting me to hear the entire tape. There must have been something incriminating to them both on it. I knew also that that was another reason Sandy had wanted the tapes back so desperately. It wasn't only political but personal too. If the news had got out, Sandy's marriage would have been on the rocks and his political career over. The PM has, after all, to be whiter than white, at least in the eyes of the public.

It had been the only possible explanation. But I was prepared to forgive them both if Pamela just confessed. I knew if she didn't, our ways would have to part and, if that happened, my whole life would unravel completely.

'What makes you think that?' she asked weakly.

'Never mind that. It's true, isn't it?' I said brutally.

'If you're so sure, why do you have to ask?'

'Because, if we are to have a future together, I think we should have no secrets,' I said.

She started crying then and, between her tears, managed to say, 'Yes, it's true. But it was only a brief fling. I think he was in lust, not love. And I was attracted by his power.'

'Not his body?' I asked, possibly even more brutally.

'Not like I am by yours,' she replied simply. 'Oh, please, Jack. I've been looking forward so much to a future together. Please forgive me.' And she started crying again even harder.

I went up to her and gave her a huge hug. 'Of course I forgive you, my darling. I love you. You know that. But let's have no more secrets, OK?'

Then we were tearing each other's clothes off and making love furiously, desperately. Afterwards I passed her a paper hankie and she blew her nose and wiped her eyes.

'So what now?' she asked.

'I'd like to ask you to become the second Mrs Sanderson,' I said.

'Oh, yes, Jack. I accept!' And we made love again. We both slept after that until dinner time. We had dinner, and then went back to bed again. I slept till the next morning.

Chapter 25 Friday and the aftermath

When I got up, I checked my mobile and saw I had a message from Sir Maurice, asking me to call him back. I did so and heard his voice say, 'Hi, Jack.'

'Hi, yourself. What news?'

'That Smythe chap has been an absolute treasure trove of information. He has given us more than I dared hope for. We can now put quite a few major criminals behind bars for a very long time. Thanks, by the way, for asking Bullock to cooperate. He has been very helpful.'

'That's OK. I'm glad you got results. What about the missing files?'

'You were quite right, Jack. Miss Burrows' file is missing too. That's the only other one, I think.'

'Maybe it will turn up in the stuff we got from his house. I think you should ask Smythe what he did with the two files. I

233

don't want them to be released into the public domain.'

'No, I appreciate that perfectly. I will do that this morning.'

'But, assuming it's been destroyed, which I think is more than likely, does it mean that she can start with a completely clean slate? After all, no one, apart from yourself, the PM and Smythe, knows her background. And I don't think any of you will be rushing to release the information.'

'In answer to your question, yes, that's exactly what it means. There is one other thing: we think we know how Smythe got to our Chief Librarian but it wasn't money this time. We just found some very indecent pornography buried deep inside a computer at his house. I will be asking Smythe about it. So you were right. He did have a secret vice like Sir Edward.'

'OK. Good on both counts. It looks like you'll need to tighten up your vetting procedures. I'll let you know about the job,' I said and hung up.

Pamela was still sleeping and I left her and went downstairs to have breakfast. She joined me quite soon and I confirmed what I had told her last night about being able to start afresh. Then I said, 'Sir Maurice has offered me my old job back.'

She looked at me and said, 'Do you really want to go back?'

'Not immediately, no. But I can't see myself pottering around a garden with a pipe and slippers until I drop dead of sheer boredom.'

'You do whatever you feel is right,' she said and I was glad to have her support.

I took her back to London in my car and, on the way, we talked about where we were going to live after the wedding. She told me that her house had been given to her in perpetuity by MI5 and that she was perfectly prepared to sell it and move in with me. I thought of my poky little flat with all its memories of Jenny and suggested that I sold that too and we bought a place of our own. She was pleased at the idea and said that it would be a new beginning for both of us. I realised that there was still so much that I didn't know about her from her financial situation to her shoe size but I was in love and left all that stuff for later.

When we got back to London, we went immediately to a jewellery shop and she chose an engagement ring, a simple platinum band set with a few small sapphires. I approved of her taste as I knew I would. Then I took her to my flat and she looked

around it with interest, summing it up succinctly as a 'typical bachelor pad', which
brought me up short until I realised that
every vestige of Jenny had disappeared.
But she agreed to move in with me anyway
and went off back to her house to collect
some of her belongings.

While she was out, I rang Sandy and
told him the news of our forthcoming wedding. He was speechless at first but, when
he found his voice, said, 'All my very best
wishes, Jack. Wait till I tell Sarah. I know
she will be delighted too.' I didn't mention
the fact that I knew of his 'little fling' with
Pamela. Then I asked him to be my best
man and he readily agreed. I knew there
were lots of preparations to set in motion
and I started by ringing Westminster Town
Hall and asking for the banns to be posted.

Pamela returned later in a taxi loaded
with her stuff and we carted it all inside. I
told her what I had done in her absence and
she looked dubious at first about Sandy
being my best man but, when I pointed out
that he was still my best friend, she came
round to the idea saying only, 'It could be
a little embarrassing, you know.'

'I'm sure he will behave impeccably,' I
said and we left it at that.

The next few weeks went by quickly. There were so many things to do: invitations to get organised, a church to be found (she insisted on that), my flat and her house to be put on the market and a million and one other things. Meanwhile we got to know each other better, not a bad thing to do before getting married, I thought wryly. I was well aware our courtship had been a whirlwind one and conducted in very strange circumstances but I also knew my choice of woman had been the right one, just as I had been sure of Jenny all those years ago. Apart from anything else, she had lived in the secret world and knew what my job had entailed. And there weren't many women around I could say that of.

The big day finally came and we got married in a small parish church in Highgate where we had found a spacious flat. We hadn't exchanged contracts yet so we were still living in my old flat but I felt it was all coming together. The wedding was fine – she had no living male relatives and had chosen Joe to give her away and be a witness which he said he was honoured to do, a lovely gesture, I thought. Sandy and Sarah duly turned up and Sandy danced with Pamela at the reception. But I wasn't jealous any more. There was nobody there from the secret world Pamela and I had so recently inhabited, just a few of my old drinking buddies from the pub local to my flat, my cleaning lady, Betty, and a few old University friends of Pamela's who seemed surprised at having been asked. So it was a small group but that suited us fine. We had decided to drive to Cornwall for our honeymoon and we left straight after the reception.

When we returned, we settled into the domestic bliss of newly-weds until one day, several months later after I'd finished writing the foregoing, I told her I was starting to get bored. She shooed me out of our new flat, telling me to go straight to Sir Maurice. I drove down to MI5 headquarters where I was greeted like the Prodigal Son by my old colleagues. I went up to the top floor and into Sir Maurice's office with its magnificent view of the river and the Houses of Parliament and said, 'Is that job offer still open?'

'Still got the fire in your belly, eh, Jack?' he said.

'I think I can still be of some use,' I replied hopefully.

'Well, as it happens, I may have a use for you,' he said, handing me a file marked Top Secret.

I moved back in at a couple of grades up as if I'd never been away and am still there.

THE END

About the Author

After leaving university in London, Richard Sloane roamed the world as a peripatetic English teacher for about twenty years, teaching an enormous variety of students up to and including university level, with just a couple of years back in England to do further studying. Then he returned to live in Cambridge and continued teaching for roughly another twenty years until he was forced to retire for medical reasons. After this he became a full-time author and has so far published seven novels for adults and a number of books for children and young people. These can be viewed on his website at: richardsloanebooks.com and are all available for purchase on Amazon.

9 781970 072778